SIMPLE SABOTAGE

SURVIVING BUREAUCRACY WITH SNARK AND STYLE

A GRIMSWORLD GUIDE BY

DAVID HANKINS

Also by David Hankins

Grimsworld

Death and the Taxman
Death and the Dragon
Death and the Immortal
(Coming 2026)

Grimsworld Tales
(Companion Collection)

Simple Sabotage:
Surviving Bureaucracy with Snark and Style

These books and more available at
www.davidhankins.com

To the Soldiers, NCOs, and Officers of the
191st Ordnance Battalion.

Thank you for teaching a naïve lieutenant
how to survive bureaucracy with snark and style.

CONTENTS

INTRODUCTION

As I write this in early 2025, I am struck by the possibility that some may not realize that this book is, in its entirety, satire wrapped in the comfort of fiction, inspired by (God help me) an actual military regulation. Some may think I am taking sides in the increasingly polarized ideologies within American politics, or British politics, or Canadian politics, or whatever political regime you may be suffering under as you read it.

I am not. I make it a point in my writing to remain apolitical, not saying that one side is better than the other regardless of which side you're on. Because, frankly, all the sides of the political spectrum (including the one I'm not taking) could stand to have a little light shed upon their various activities.

And that is the point of my brand of satire. To shed a little light and to laugh at the silliness we face every day while suffering under the most evil, pernicious, and unremitting form of government management in the entire world: Bureaucracy.

A little history about me: I served in the United States Army for twenty years as a logistics officer, surviving one of the biggest bureaucracies in the world through sheer stubbornness until I could retire. I deployed once to Afghanistan, twice to Iraq, received two Bronze Stars, a number of lesser awards (because bureaucracies love giving awards to demonstrate their benevolence), and retired as soon as I could. During that time, I served under some amazing leaders, some complete jerks, and a few individuals who epitomized the caricature of 'bureaucrat' presented herein. All in all, I found most of my fellow soldiers (and the civilian employees who supported us) to be decent human beings. We all did the best we could within the bureaucratic system we suffered under.

The title and text of this book were inspired by the *Simple Sabotage Field Manual* published on January 17th, 1944, by the Office of Strategic Services (Provisional) and declassified by the Central Intelligence Agency on April 2nd, 2008. Yes, I realize that I'm probably on some watchlist simply for accessing that manual on the CIA.gov website. Such are the dangers of poking a finger in the eye of bureaucracy. You can join me on the watchlist and download the original text, or simply read to the end of this book for what I consider to be the most interesting excerpts from the original *Simple Sabotage Field Manual*. I didn't include the full text because approximately half of it genuinely reads like an insurrectionist guide to destroying infrastructure, something more applicable to its time during World War II. If that's what you're looking for, head on over to the CIA.gov website.

I found the original *Simple Sabotage Field Manual* quite instructive in two ways. First, it provided simple yet actionable instructions for resisting the bureaucracy when it turns bad (really, was it ever good?) designed for the untrained layperson to execute. Second, though I know this wasn't the original intent of the manual, it outlines what bad bureaucracy looks like. Sure, this image was presented as a series of instructions for an oppressed organizational supervisor to resist Nazi occupation, but it doesn't take a lot of imagination to realize that those activities describe *exactly* what we suffer under every day in our corporate and government jobs. (e.g. "Hold conferences when there is more critical work to be done," or "To lower morale ...

discriminate against efficient workers.")

The manual was written over eighty years ago, and in the years since we (society as a whole) have embraced the bureaucratic horrors outlined within it. I don't like horror stories, especially when real life sometimes reads like the opening chapters of a dystopian thriller, so I wrote *Simple Sabotage: Surviving Bureaucracy with Snark and Style* as a bit of lighthearted satire to help myself deal with the world at large.

One final note on genre. The Grimsworld series is humorous contemporary fantasy centered around the Grim Reaper. He just wants to do his job and shepherd souls into the afterlife, but Hell's Bureaucracy, the Auditor, and the Office of Micromanagement tend to get in his way. (Yes, Hell invented bureaucracy. How else do you think it could remain so insidiously and charmingly evil after all these centuries?). If you'd like to read the Grimsworld series, I recommend starting with *Death and the Taxman,* winner of the 2024 BOOK OF THE YEAR FOR OUTSTANDING HUMOR/COMEDY/SATIRE from the Independent Author Network and BEST SCIENCE FICTION AND FANTASY NOVEL OF 2024 from the Critters Readers Poll.

What were we talking about? Oh, yeah. Genre. This is not your traditional guidebook. It doesn't provide recipe-style directions for surviving bureaucracy. Nor, as the name might imply, is it a guide to the characters and settings of Grimsworld. It is, instead, a blending of short story collection and commentary on the original *Simple Sabotage Field Manual*, a bit of satire from which you can draw your own conclusions. Because, sadly, there are no simple solutions to surviving bureaucracy. But you *can* do it with snark and style. The stories are told from the perspective of Samuel Davidson, a character in my Grimsworld series. Not all of them have fantasy elements, but all are heavily seasoned with details drawn from my decades of government service. One of the stories is drawn full cloth from my life with only the names and a few minor details changed to protect the innocent. No, I'm not telling you which one.

Happy reading!

David Hankins

THE BLUE TOWEL INCIDENT

"Insist on doing everything through channels. Never permit shortcuts to be taken in order to expedite decisions. Apply all regulations to the last letter."
— The Simple Sabotage Field Manual

There are few things more terrifying than being yelled at by a naked, dripping-wet lieutenant colonel. LTC Napoli was a small man, both in stature and personality, whose greatest joys in life came from using Army regulations like a sledgehammer to prove that he was right. And, Sam was sad to admit, he often was. He also had no sense of humor when it came to himself. Yet, LTC Napoli was quick with the barbed comment or hooting laugh whenever any of his staff messed up.

Heaven help the staffer who tried to give tit for tat.

Sam's day had started so well. September mornings in the mountains of Afghanistan were often chilly, heavy dew glistening in the sharp, clear sunrise. The air was crisp with that clean high-desert smell of sand and scrub brush. If Sam closed his eyes, he could almost imagine he was in eastern Montana instead of Afghanistan. Despite being in a warzone, mornings on their Forward Operating Base were usually peaceful.

The recently promoted Captain Samuel Davidson had finished his morning run and was looking forward to a nice warm shower before the daily Battle Update Brief to LTC Napoli. Not that a logistics battalion had much battle to update, but that's the term the combat units used, so they did too.

Sam slowly climbed the rickety metal stairs up to the showers. Life on a FOB didn't have a lot of comforts, but whoever had installed the showers in Sam's little slice of heaven knew their plumbing. He couldn't say the same for their basic engineering skills.

The stairs shivered under his weight, the trip up to the shower possibly being the most dangerous thing he'd do today. After Sam's promotion to captain, LTC Napoli moved him from platoon leader to battalion adjutant to oversee all aspects of personnel administration. As little more than a glorified admin clerk, Sam's greatest danger every day—aside from the stairs even now threatening to collapse underneath him—was risk of a concussion from falling asleep at his desk.

The showers were on the second floor of a Frankenstein's Monster of a building constructed out of cross-stacked, rusty twenty-foot shipping containers called MILVANs. Two MILVANs on the ground were retrofitted with bathrooms, one each for males and females, with the showers up above. Gravity-fed water tanks squatted atop the horrendous masterpiece of rust and repurposed sheet metal like misplaced elephants.

The stairs didn't kill him today, and Sam's shower was everything he needed: hot and with decent pressure. This was going to be a good day, he just knew it.

Then Sam stepped out of the shower.

High-pitched rage reverberated around the tiny metal room. Five soldiers in various stages of undress were frozen in shock as the diminutive, freshly showered, and completely naked LTC Napoli stood nose to chest with the beanpole known as SGT Cooper, screaming into the poor sergeant's face. Despite his height advantage, Cooper—who was also naked, Sam couldn't help but notice—looked like a rabbit ready to bolt from an enraged terrier. LTC Napoli's finger jabbed almost up SGT Cooper's nose. He screamed accusations of theft most heinous.

Somebody had stolen the commander's blue towel while he was showering.

Sam resisted smiling as he dried off. Soldiers love pulling pranks, and as far as pranks go, this one was delightfully simple and didn't hurt anyone—a key consideration. Sam mentally tipped his hat to the boss's saboteur.

The subject of LTC Napoli's wrath didn't appear to share Sam's amusement. SGT Cooper's expression was somewhere between horror at the screaming naked man before him, and terror at his future prospects for a promising career. Of the potential suspects in the room, Sam wouldn't have picked SGT Cooper. He was a quiet soul with the gentle disposition of the terminally non-confrontational. Sam had no idea how he'd managed to achieve the rank of sergeant.

Unfortunately, the good sergeant's towel was blue, a damning bit of evidence. Between accusations from his enraged commander, SGT Cooper managed to stammer,

"This is m-my towel, Sir. Got my name on it." He presented the edge of his towel with his name emblazoned in black marker, a common precaution when you couldn't guarantee the laundry you got back was actually yours.

LTC Napoli glared then spun on the next soldier, voice high and tinny against the metal walls. "Did you steal my towel?"

"No sir." The soldier presented a white towel as evidence.

"You?" the boss whirled again. Water droplets flew.

"No sir," came the next response. This continued until Sam was forced to hold up his towel—brown—as evidence of his innocence. He certainly hadn't pulled the prank, he'd been in the shower while the mysterious thief worked his magic. Unconvinced, the boss shoved his naked way around the room, examining every corner, crouching to search under every bench.

His blue towel was gone.

Tense silence fell as the commander dried off with the paper towels beside the sink, cursing and mumbling the entire time. Soldiers and NCOs quietly showered. Sam dressed as fast as he could before fleeing down the rickety stairs. That had been the most bizarre yet hilarious morning Sam could remember since arriving in Afghanistan. The rusted steel quivered under his steps as though sharing in his barely contained laughter.

***

It should have ended there. The unspoken rules of the prank are clear. If you're the victim, you rant and rave and curse the heavens, then give in and chuckle at the daring audacity of your prankster. After things have died down, the prankster returns what was taken, perhaps confesses over a shared cup of joe if they're feeling brave, and everybody enjoys a nice laugh. Then life goes on, the victim of the prank planning their retaliation if they identified the mastermind behind their brief embarrassment.

That sounds great in theory, but for one fact: LTC Napoli wouldn't let it go.

The morning BUB was a farce. The staff tried in vain to brief their various topics, every slide becoming a platform for LTC Napoli to complain about his stolen blue towel. What should have taken a mere thirty minutes became a two-hour rant about honor and respect to a staff who, aside from Sam, hadn't been anywhere near the scene of the crime. The BUB ended when the boss directed Command Sergeant Major O'Toole to email the *entire* battalion, demanding the thief come forward. Confess his crime and accept his punishment.

Reluctantly, CSM O'Toole—a connoisseur of the prank himself—did so.

To nobody's surprise, nobody came forward. Terror at the commander's simmering wrath, however, did work its evil magic on SGT Cooper.

Sam slumped in his uncomfortable folding chair inside the clapboard adjutant's office. Buildings on the FOB were nothing more than plywood and two-by-fours. He was sipping his third cup of coffee and pondering the case when motion caught his eye. It was nearing lunchtime, but someone was coming in, not out. SGT Cooper slipped furtively past. He looked guilty and clutched a plastic shopping bag in his arms.

What was this? Sam arched an intrigued eyebrow. LTC Napoli was out, so he rose to follow the sergeant.

CSM O'Toole reached him first. Sam entered the commander's office to find Cooper braced at parade rest before the sergeant major, the now-empty plastic bag behind his back. The senior NCO noticed Sam in the doorway but kept his focus on Cooper.

"What the hell is this?" CSM O'Toole growled, indicating a blue towel on the commander's desk. It still had a price tag from the shoppette on it.

"I, uh," stammered the sergeant before his shoulders drooped, "LTC Napoli said I took his towel."

"Did you?"

"No! But, he thinks I did it, and he yelled at me. I don't want more trouble."

The sergeant major sighed. "So, you bought him a new towel?"

Cooper nodded. CSM O'Toole rolled his eyes heavenward then gestured grandly at the towel. "*This* isn't the way to avoid an ass chewing. If LTC Napoli finds out you brought this in, he'll crucify you!" The sergeant major grabbed the towel and shoved it into SGT Cooper's arms so roughly that the sergeant stumbled back. "Get out of here before the boss sees you. Go on, git!"

SGT Cooper scurried from the office, barely pausing for a polite, "Sir," as he slid past Sam. CSM O'Toole watched him go, shaking his head and chuckling.

"So," Sam asked, "who do you think did it?" He sipped his coffee.

The sergeant major shrugged, a smile playing at the corner of his lips. "Don't know, don't care. But it'll be fun to see how this all pans out."

***

It all panned out with Sam taking the brunt of LTC Napoli's wrath.

A month later was Halloween. The mystery of the blue towel remained unsolved and was a source of amused—though quiet—speculation among the staff. It became something of a game to 'accidentally' get the boss riled up over the incident, especially at meetings that turned boring. Yes, it was a warzone, and they did focus on the job of supporting the warfighters with the best logistics they could, but not a lot happened on the FOB itself. So, the staff sought amusement where they could find it.

As the boss prepared for his R&R leave—a free two-week trip home that every soldier received during the year-long deployment to Afghanistan—someone came up with the idea of throwing a Halloween costume party while he was gone. A chance for the mice to play while the cat was away.

Sam wasn't skilled at designing costumes from random clothing items, scissors, and thread, but an idea came to him over his morning coffee. Something that everyone would laugh at.

Well, almost everyone.

Halloween arrived cold, dark, and spooky. For the party, they'd cleared the furniture out of one of the plywood huts they lived in, dimmed the lights, cranked the music, and set out an eclectic assortment of snacks and pop. Parties down range—i.e. in locations where people like to shoot at you—weren't the same as back home. Alcohol wasn't allowed, supplies were limited, and everybody had to carry their assigned weapon regardless of uniform or lack there-of. It was truly bizarre to see werewolves, Dracula, and even jolly old Saint Nick sidle into the building armed to the teeth. Santa's drum-fed M249 SAW made Sam worry about the kids on the naughty list. But not too much. This was the Army way.

The party was in full swing. Sam swaggered through the door wearing a pair of boxers, LTC Napoli's uniform blouse—which he'd borrowed from the boss's laundry bag before he went on R&R—and his pistol slung low on his hip like an old-West gunslinger.

A blue towel draped his shoulders.

The room exploded with laughter. Sam grinned as CSM O'Toole strolled up in full uniform, his only nod to the season a pair of devil horns fashioned out of tin foil. The sergeant major looked Sam up and down, nodding in appreciation.

"Well done, Captain."

"LTC Napoli, I think you mean." Sam thrust his shoulders back and slipped his fingers between the buttons of his blouse, the perfect caricature of Napoleon striking a pose.

"Indeed," O'Toole nodded. "But I'm not sure the commander will appreciate—"

Over the music, somebody yelled, "Say 'cheese'!" Sam glanced over just in time to be blinded by a camera flash.

"—your sense of humor," the sergeant major finished.

Sam shrugged off the comment. "Come on, first round's on me!"

"Actually, it's on the Army," the CSM said. "I'm pretty sure those crates under the table are from the dining facility."

"Crates?" Sam said. "What … oh, those crates!" He was all wide-eyed innocence. "Well, the DFAC serves soldiers, and that's all I see here. Except for Saint Nick, but you wouldn't begrudge a jolly old man his"—Sam squinted in the dim light—"Rip It Energy Drink and Oreos, would you?" CSM O'Toole chuckled and shook his head. Sam steered him to the 'bar' to peruse the selection of soft drinks.

The music rolled over them and, for a brief moment Sam found himself imagining that he was back home. It was a good feeling. He focused on the snacks, searching for the Oreos.

He should have paid attention to the photographer.

***

A week later, LTC Napoli returned from leave. Within five minutes of his return, Sam was in his office braced at attention. Apparently, the boss had enlisted—or more likely browbeaten—SGT Cooper into 'keeping an eye out' while he was gone. So, the good sergeant did what he was told, snapped a picture of Sam's costume, and emailed it to the boss.

That ass-chewing was one for the books. LTC Napoli was so loud that soldiers two buildings over could hear him, or so Sam was told later. He railed about honor and respect, accusing Sam of everything from Conduct Unbecoming an Officer to Disrespecting a Senior Officer to Theft.

Sam stood rigid before the commander's desk. "Sir," he injected into a lull in the yelling, "if I'm being charged with a crime, you have to read me my rights."

"What?" LTC Napoli said, taken aback.

"Am I being charged under the Uniform Code of Military Justice, Sir? Because if I am, according to the UCMJ I have a right to know the charges, speak with my attorney, and present my defense in court."

The commander chewed his lip. "For your flagrant disregard of military decorum and the *theft* of my uniform ... Yes, I am considering an Article 15."

Ah, non-judicial punishment. Enough to dock some pay, assign extra duty ... and end Sam's career. No officer with an Article 15 in their file ever got promoted. Sam nodded.

"I do not believe the case will stand up in court, Sir," Sam said, eyes boring a hole into the plywood wall two inches above LTC Napoli's head, "As your laundry was returned with all items accounted for." Sam had been careful about that.

"Court?" The commander's eyes widened slightly as if in surprise that Sam was standing up for himself.

"Sir, per Section V, Paragraph 3 of the UCMJ, the accused may demand a trial by court-martial, and as the accused, I feel that I have a strong defense against the charges laid. Whether I do or not will be up to the judge once the full details of the case have been laid forth by the lawyers."

LTC Napoli sat back. His eyes narrowed. He was angry, but he wasn't stupid. An Article 15 could be handled quietly in-house, a way to finally vent his anger over being embarrassed by the whole blue towel incident, Sam's career be damned. A court-martial, however, would tell the world of his embarrassment. Sam waited, unsure of which direction the boss would go, to see if he would choose his fragile ego over his burning need to be right.

"A court-martial is a lot of paperwork," LTC Napoli said and drummed his fingers on his desk. "Yet you clearly have no concept of what honor and respect mean, Captain. So, in lieu of pursuing punishment under the UCMJ, I want you to write an essay of seven thousand words on the subject. You have two days."

An essay? Like he was in high school? Sam considered

quibbling, but he knew that he'd won. This was just LTC Napoli's way of saving face. Besides, Sam knew a *lot* about the topic. He'd done a research project on the evolution of honor codes in college. All he needed to do was tweak it a little to add shaded comments about the honor implications of belittling subordinates, and it would be perfect. He would even, quietly, share it among the staff. To ensure they were fully conversant on the topic, of course.

Sam saluted smartly. "Yes, Sir," he said, then dropped his salute and left with only one question still burning in his mind.

Who the *hell* stole the blue towel in the first place? Sam really wanted to shake the man's hand.

SAMUEL DAVIDSON'S WAR

"Snarl up administration in every possible way. Fill out forms illegibly so that they will have to be done over; make mistakes or omit requested information in forms. Give lengthy and incomprehensible explanations when questioned."

– The Simple Sabotage Field Manual

War is hell, but government bureaucracy in the middle of a war? That was the epitome of evil.

At least, that was what Sam used to think, back in the good old days before he came face-to-face with real evil. Before he'd met his personally assigned demon from Hell's Department of Bureaucratic Torments.

Yes, that Hell. The one with wailing and gnashing of

teeth and, apparently, forms in quadruplicate. It all started on his fifth deployment to sunny Iraq. Samuel Davidson had joined the U.S. Army as an optimistic second lieutenant with dreams of seeing the world while defending democracy in pursuit of life, liberty, and justice.

What a fool he'd been.

Nineteen years later, Sam was a disgruntled career staff officer counting the days until retirement. He should have read the fine print when he commissioned. Yeah, he'd seen the world, but not the parts with sunny beaches and fruity drinks sporting paper umbrellas. He'd suffered through back-to-back government-funded vacations to sandbox-es and jungles with bad food, angry locals, and less than one-star accommodations in places few people ever heard of. Hell, the current war in Iraq had been going on so long that folks back home had practically forgotten it was still a thing. News only reached the front page when some new atrocity sent a busload of innocents to the afterlife. Soldiers and civilians died every day out there, and nobody seemed to care.

Not that Sam did any of the actual fighting. As the Division Logistics Officer, his biggest battle was an ongoing fight with the Division Operations Officer, Colonel Patton over the dubious merits of PowerPoint in a warzone. Old Blood and Guts Patton from WWII was probably rolling in his grave to have such an idiot serving with the same name.

Sam was a logistician trained in the fine art of getting the right stuff to the right person on time every time. One did not win wars with PowerPoint. COL Patton disagreed. And because he was the senior staff officer and the commanding general's golden child, his word was law.

The division conference room was a cramped, windowless hole featuring a hand-carved mahogany table surrounded by folding chairs. The original chairs had been 'acquired' by soldiers years ago in the age-old military tradition of redistributing resources to whoever had the stickiest fingers. The table remained only because nobody could figure out how to disassemble it to get it out the door. What had once been an opulent Iraqi government facility was now shabby and crumbling. Years of military occupation had taken its toll.

It was also hotter than the Devil's armpit and smelled even worse. The AC had died a rattling, wheezing death just that morning.

Sam slouched in his hard, battered folding chair as slide

number seventy-two flipped onto the screen at the end of the table. The Assistant Public Affairs Officer rose from his chair against the back wall. He was a skinny, bespectacled captain in whom nature had seen fit to combine a deep orator's voice with a complete lack of social skills. Listening to his briefings was like having Paul Harvey read the back of a cereal box.

As the PAO said exactly the same things he'd said yesterday and probably would tomorrow, Sam took a long draught of his coffee. He drank hot coffee even on the desert's most sweltering days. It was the only thing that kept him sane.

On those rare days when Army idiocy didn't get in the way, Sam actually liked his job. He was good at it. And there was nothing more satisfying than knowing that he'd helped the guys at the sharp end of the stick live a little bit longer.

COL Patton caught Sam's eye from across the table and arched an eyebrow. With a persecuted sigh, Sam sat up straight and gave every impression of paying attention. As he pretended to be a dutiful subordinate, visions of a job in the civilian sector danced in his mind. One without idiots and red tape.

Sam suppressed a snort. No, that was asking too much. Idiots and red tape are universal.

The PAO's sonorous voice droned on. There wasn't enough coffee in the world to make this bearable.

"The representative from the Center of Military History arrived this morning," the PAO said, "here to inventory the artifact cache Second Brigade found last month. LTC Diaz said she's looking for some cataloging assistance. Should take about a week. If anybody would like to volunteer—"

Sam's hand shot into the air before his brain caught up with it.

"Lieutenant Colonel Davidson?" COL Patton asked threateningly. He didn't like people interrupting his meetings.

"I'm in!" Sam said after a mere half-second's thought. "I mean, I'd be happy to volunteer for this vital mission in support of the war effort." If it got him out of attending these meetings for a week, Sam would have volunteered to work in the burn pit.

Okay, maybe not that. The burn pit was where they immolated the base's trash, a nasty hole in the ground whose tar-black plume probably contained enough carcinogens to rival the fallout from Chernobyl. If he wanted that level of toxicity, he'd just hang out around COL Patton.

"Noted," Patton growled. They'd never gotten along. Apparently sarcastic commentary about, well, everything was not 'appropriate behavior' for a senior staff officer and Sam needed to 'grow up.'

Yeah, he'd get right on that.

The glare COL Patton leveled at Sam could have spontaneously combusted dry ice. Sam grinned back and sipped his coffee. With a grunt, the Ops Officer nodded at the PAO to continue. Slide number seventy-three slid onto the screen.

***

Sam had no idea how one became an Army Historian. It's not like 'Historian' was one of the options dangled before young Cadet Davidson before the Army volun-told him to be a logistician. He'd expected a drab, lifeless bureaucrat but was pleasantly surprised to find that LTC Karmi Diaz—who insisted he call her Karmi—was a gregarious, charming, chatty Puerto Rican who loved her job. That last fact was enough to make Sam reconsider his life choices. He'd never met an officer who actually *had fun* working for Uncle Sam as a senior officer. Sure, a lot of officers Sam knew had drunk the Kool-Aid, but they just became driven to the point of burnout—either their own or their subordinates. 'Fun' wasn't part of the job.

It was for Karmi.

Under her delightful direction, Sam threw himself into inventorying expensive art and weird artifacts that Saddam had squirreled away before the invasion. Karmi had set up shop in an old Iraqi hangar on the backside of the airfield. It wasn't air-conditioned but remained surprisingly cool despite the sweltering desert heat outside. Old crates of artifacts lined one wall, several tables sat in the center, and new empty crates lined the opposite wall. For six days Sam arrived early and stayed late, working and chatting with the charming historian. It was, by far, the most enjoyable week Sam could remember in the desert. And best of all—no death by PowerPoint.

Sam knew—and Karmi confirmed—that the artifacts belonged to the Iraqi people, or at least to their new government once they had one. But after foreign insurgents intentionally destroyed several ancient historical sites, the Army had decided to warehouse everything they found of historic value back at the Smithsonian. Once peace was achieved—a distant day, Sam feared—everything would be returned. Or so they claimed.

It was their last day of inventories. Karmi was overseeing the crating of some Persian vases while Sam busily inventoried the last few items on his table. The description field on the Army inventory form was small, so Sam had to tighten his handwriting.

Item number 186: Platter, golden, one each. Dancing naked virgins around edge. Third virgin with nice smile. Sam smirked. He'd added little bits of snark and commentary to each item he'd inventoried. He hoped that whoever opened these crates back in DC had a sense of humor.

Item number 187: Jeweled Dagger, ceremonial, one each. Super creepy demon head on pommel. Sheath more gemstone-studded than Elton John's glasses. Sam slid the dagger from its obscenely bejeweled sheath. *Obsidian blade, no chips.* He slid his right thumb across the blade. He hadn't pressed hard, but the dagger cut deep.

"Ack!" Sam snapped his thumb back, flinging blood. "Son of a bi—scuit eater!" He'd been trying for years to curb his swearing—more than one commander had dressed him down for it—but *damn* that hurt. He sucked on his thumb as he picked up the pen in his left hand. With a wobbly scrawl, he wrote, *Sharp as sh—*

Sam stopped himself from writing obscenities on an official Army form. Barely. While properly applied profanity felt good at the moment, it didn't have the impact he was looking for. Sam pulled his bleeding thumb from his mouth, considering it. Blood oozed from the small but deep cut. With a feral smile and a chuckle, Sam pressed his thumb to the form.

That should do it. '*Sharp as* BLOODY THUMBPRINT' made a much bolder statement.

Sam grabbed a nearby rag and applied pressure to his thumb before sheathing the dagger. He could swear that the smirking demon head on the pommel was laughing at him. Sam stuck out his tongue at it before wrapping it up and slipping it into the crate.

"That's it!" he called to Karmi, who jogged over to shake his hand. Sam's grip was a bit awkward with the rag wrapped around his thumb, but they managed.

"Thank you so much for your help," she said, pumping his hand hard enough to rattle his shoulder. "When I asked for volunteers, I expected to get privates and specialists given extra duty for screwing up. Your assistance was a godsend. If you need anything, don't hesitate to call."

Sam returned her handshake with matching gusto, unsure what kind of emergency would require a historian's assistance.

He soon found out.

***

Sam sauntered unhurriedly back across the base, moving with the pedestrian flow as folks made their way toward the chow hall for dinner. It might have felt like strolling through downtown Albuquerque if everyone weren't carrying weapons and dressed in military uniforms. Although to be fair, only half the people were armed. Contractors and civilian government employees weren't allowed firearms, even in the warzone.

Sam whistled tunelessly to himself, enjoying the afterglow of an entire week spent without a single PowerPoint slide. He doubted they'd even missed him back at Division HQ. It wasn't like he was vital to some decisive operation. There were no decisive operations these days. The Army just sent units on back-to-back deployments so soldiers could flounder around trying to establish democracy in a country that didn't want it—soldiers whose only skillset lay in blowing things up, not winning hearts and minds. The locals had been repelling invaders for centuries and had gotten pretty good at it.

Sam shook his head. He needed to retire and find some cushy corporate gig. What would it be like to work somewhere that people weren't actively trying to kill you? Hell, perhaps he'd even start dating. Continuous deployments hadn't been good for Sam's love life.

Sirens wailed to life; incoming rockets launched by the locals for the third time that day. Sam didn't even twitch. You can get used to anything. He was supposed to run for the concrete bunkers scattered around the base, and a few folks around him did just that. But this base was big enough and the rockets were random enough that the chances of getting hit were astronomically low. Plus, the base's fancy new counter-rocket Gatling guns were really good at shooting down anything bigger and faster than a dove. Sam glanced skyward, shielded his eyes from the sun, and hoped for some good fireworks.

BOOM!

Sam jumped when the rocket impacted a hundred yards away. Sand and rocks erupted skyward. The shockwave slammed into Sam, blowing his hat off.

BOOM!

That one was even closer, the shockwave knocking Sam onto his butt. Shrapnel whizzed past before embedding itself into the sand, the sidewalk, and a spindly palm tree.

Shit. If there was ever a time to swear, this was it.

Sam abruptly realized that he was alone out in the open. He sprinted for the nearest bunker. It was large and T-shaped with three entrances. The foot-thick concrete could withstand anything beyond a direct hit. He bolted inside and—

BOOM!

The third rocket impacted just outside the bunker. The blast blew Sam against the cement back wall. Stars flashed. He gasped for breath. Abrupt ringing in his ears drowned everything in a cacophony of silence. His legs turned watery and Sam slid down the wall like a cartoon character. When his senses returned, he found himself collapsed amidst a tumble of terrified soldiers and civilians. Nearest was a female major who was practically fetal on the gravel. She was wide-eyed with her hands clasped over her ears, mouth open in a scream Sam couldn't hear over the ringing in his own ears. Sand and cordite from the blast filled the air. It made oddly pretty swirls as hot wind blew through the bunker.

Sam shakily rolled to his knees and checked himself for holes. Everything hurt but seemed intact. He'd need a double dose of Motrin after today.

"Well, aren't you the lucky one," a weaselly voice said, barely audible over the piccolo playing in Sam's inner ear.

He glanced around. Only the major was looking at him, though he doubted she saw him. She was glassy-eyed with terror. Everybody else had their eyes squeezed shut, arms covering their heads as they waited for the next impact. Sam was surprised to see COL Patton amidst the huddled masses, the only face he recognized.

Sam blinked and shook his head, trying to clear it. That voice hadn't been the major's. It had been male. He opened his mouth wide to try and pop his ears.

"I could have sworn that third rocket would get you," the voice continued. "Well, maybe next time."

Someone small behind the major moved. Sam shifted aside to see them. He froze in surprise.

It was … a demon. Only two feet tall and with a rumpled business suit, he might have passed as a small human, but the red eyes and little horns poking through his greasy combover were a dead giveaway.

Sam's brain lurched. Demons weren't real. Sure, he'd gone to Sunday school and heard all the sermons, but he'd never really *believed.* But here was this … thing with his clawed hand *inside* the major's head, stirring her fear as though stirring soup.

This was it; Sam had finally gone crazy.

His gibbering hindbrain clawed control from his fore-brain, which happily surrendered, though with a snarky reminder that *demons aren't real.* His pistol appeared in his hand. Sam aimed, conscious thought playing no part as his finger found the trigger. "Demon!" he yelled.

The major's glassy-eyed expression abruptly focused. A pistol pointed in your direction tends to do that. She launched herself into Sam. Her hand slapped the pistol aside before she body-slammed him into the wall.

BANG!

The pistol fired toward the bunker entrance. The major's knee found Sam's gut while her hands wrapped around his. She twisted her grip, Sam gasped, and suddenly he was staring down his own weapon. Smoke drifted upward from the barrel.

Sam fought for breath, eyes focused on the pistol mere

inches from his face. Behind the major, the demon cocked his head to one side. Sam met his gaze and the demon's eyes widened.

"Hold up, sunshine ... you can see me?" the little imp said. Mutely, Sam nodded. A look of unmitigated joy filled that hideous face, but then Sam's attention was wrenched back to the major.

"Hands up!" she yelled.

Sam belatedly realized that she was wearing a Military Police tabard. He raised his hands. She whipped a pair of handcuffs from her back pocket. Sam slumped as she proceeded with the inevitable.

***

The next three months were pure hell. The full force of the Army's bureaucratic machine came down on one LTC Samuel Davidson like an avalanche. Cops led to lawyers who led to a very sour-faced judge who led to shrinks. They brought him back to his duty station of Fort Carson, Colorado for trial and to determine if Sam was nuts or a cold-blooded killer, the soul of evil hellbent on murdering Soldiers like the prosecution claimed. COL Patton was their prize witness who helped shape that narrative.

Sam knew he wasn't the bad guy, but he wasn't entirely sure about the state of his own mind. He *had* seen the demon. Hadn't he? The little fiend had examined Sam like a rare delicacy during the arrest, circling him and poking him as if confirming that Sam's third eye was indeed open. Then Hell's greasiest minion had disappeared without a trace.

Sam might have chalked the whole incident up to post traumatic stress or even just spending too much time in the blistering desert sun, but for one fact: he was still seeing demons. There weren't many, but once you'd seen one, you knew the signs. A pair of horns amidst the courtroom reporters, red eyes that burned into your soul, or a smile that revealed sharp, pointed teeth. Sam never engaged with them, kept his gaze averted, but he knew they were there.

Like the demon who hovered attentively behind his psychiatrist's shoulder. The shrink's office was dark and comfortable with the classic fainting couch for patients and a leather armchair for the doc. The demon was androgynous, thin, and lanky with thick glasses and a nervous twitch.

Which was a decent description of Dr. Smallwood too.

They had matching slicked-back hair.

"The small demon you describe," Smallwood said with a honey-smooth voice, "sounds like a classic caricature of your fears."

Sam snorted. He was reclined on the obscenely comfortable couch, arms crossed, gaze fixed on the dark oak ceiling. "You're saying I'm afraid of little people? I haven't met enough of them to form an opinion. The Army is rather sizeist in its recruiting restrictions."

"You're deflecting with sarcasm again," the doc's annoyed sigh was palpable, "I meant bureaucrats. They are your greatest fear."

Sam twitched. That ... actually hit close to home. He hated bureaucrats with a passion—an opinion that hadn't improved with his ongoing court martial. Was it too far a leap to say that he also *feared* bureaucrats? Not that all of them were bad. His defense lawyer had convinced the judge that Sam wasn't a flight risk, expanding his pre-trial restrictions from an eight-by-eight cell to the entirety of Fort Carson. The ankle monitor was annoying though.

Sam opened his mouth to respond but was interrupted.

"And that's our time for today." Dr. Smallwood rose. "As I'm sure you're aware, this was our final session."

"Great." Sam pushed himself off the couch, keeping his gaze firmly away from the demon hovering behind the shrink's shoulder. "So, what are my chances of a clean bill of health?"

"I shall provide my official findings to the judge in the morning." That wasn't an answer, but the doc waved Sam toward the door. He shoved his hands into his uniform pockets—a small but intentional breach of military etiquette—and slumped out of the office.

Sam retrieved his cell phone from the receptionist. A dozen texts and two missed calls. Sam's heart skipped a beat when he skimmed the texts. Karmi Diaz had finally called him back! He'd been trying to reach her since the trial started to ask about that stupid cursed dagger with the demon's head. Her last text said that she was in Fort Carson for a few days and asked if he'd like to meet.

Sam hit the door at a run, already dialing her number.

***

They met at Iron Horse Park in the middle of Fort Carson. The leaves were just starting to turn, adding a bit of happy orange to the park's mostly brown tone of dead grass and dirt paths. Karmi smiled broadly and waved as Sam strolled up to her park bench with two large coffees. She was wearing civies: a puffy blue jacket over slacks, her black hair contained by a knit scarf and hat. Her shoes looked expensive.

"Sorry I didn't reach out sooner," she said, taking her coffee, "I only just got your emails yesterday, right before my flight here." Karmi sipped from the hot cup. "Mmm, thank you."

Sam cocked his head. "You've been out of the office for three months?"

She nodded. "I was ... somewhere without reliable network access. But the artifacts I retrieved were worth it."

Sam wrapped both hands around his paper cup, enjoying the warmth as the breeze cut through his uniform jacket. "Wild adventures in far-flung regions just to retrieve ancient relics? You sound like Indiana Jones."

"Perhaps, but without the whip. My husband's not into that."

Sam's coffee stopped halfway to his lips. "Um..."

Karmi smiled broadly, clearly enjoying his embarrassment. Then her smile dropped. "I looked up your case. Details in the news are thin. So, how the hell did you end up on trial for attempted murder, and how is that connected to your rather frantic messages about an old Persian dagger we found in Iraq?"

Sam drew a deep breath. Nobody had believed him yet, not even the shrink, though Smallwood had presented a professionally obtuse disbelief. He drank some coffee, and told Karmi her everything. When he finished, she just shook her head.

"Heaven save us from fools," she said.

Sam blinked. "That's ... not quite the response I expected."

Karmi gave him a piercing look. "In answer to your question that was somewhere in that mess of an explanation: yes, that artifact opened your third eye. Slicing your hand with a cursed dagger before signing your name in blood is part of an ancient rite that you—like a fool—stumbled into."

"But I didn't sign anything important. It was a government form, not some infernal contract with the Devil."

Karmi arched an eyebrow and pointed with her hand that was holding the coffee cup. "You've been in the Army long enough to know that *every* government form is an infernal contract. They even come with fine print at the bottom that nobody reads."

"Sooo ... did I sell my soul or something?"

She shook her head. A bit of black hair teased free of her scarf and fluttered in the breeze. "My degrees are in history and psychology. I'm not a priest or theologian. But from what I've read, it takes a direct bargain with one of Hell's minions to sell your soul."

Sam grunted. "You sound like you actually believe all this spiritual malarkey."

"I've seen too much not to believe."

"Is there any way to close my third eye?"

"Not my area of expertise." Karmi sat back and shrugged. "Try a priest or a shaman or something."

They sat in silence for a while, watching as the autumn breeze pulled leaves from the nearby stand of maples.

"So, what happens next?" Karmi finally asked. Sam took a fortifying swig of coffee before answering.

"If doc tells the judge tomorrow that I'm not crazy, then I go to Leavenworth for entirely too many years. If he says I *am* crazy, then I get upgraded to a padded cell."

"What if you could get something ... in between?"

"Like what, a half-padded cell? I fired my weapon at an officer in front of witnesses. They're not going to let me walk."

Karmi rolled her eyes. "Sounds like acute onset PTSD to me, triggered by a near-death experience. You were, in more simple terms, only temporarily crazy."

"I'm not crazy!" Sam yelled.

"I know that, and you know that. But the court needs a believable reason why you acted as you did. It's like anything else in government service, spin a plausible story and stick with it and you can get around almost any bureaucratic hurdle. The key is unshakable confidence that your version of the truth is *the* truth. So, you had acute onset PTSD, and all you'll need are outpatient therapy and avoidance of warzone activities to be right as rain." Sam stared at her. "At least, that's what I'll tell the judge when your lawyer puts me on the stand tomorrow."

"When my ... what? When did that happen?"

"Why do you think I'm in Fort Carson? Your lawyer found me and pulled me out of the field to serve as a character witness. With my degree in psychology, I can also offer a professional counter-opinion to whatever Dr. Smallwood says. Consider this our consultation, and the coffee," Karmi smiled, "your fee."

Sam blinked a few times as he wrapped his head around

that. "Are you going to tell them about my open third eye?"

"Hell no! They'd never believe me anyway."

Sam considered his coffee, his words a sudden lump in his throat. "Thank you, Karmi. You don't know me that well, we only worked together for a week, but…"

Karmi waved away Sam's thanks. "I know good people when I meet them. Just keep your chin up tomorrow, no matter what happens."

Sam swore that he would.

***

Remaining positive in court was difficult. Nobody argued that Sam hadn't pulled the trigger—least of all him. There were too many witnesses to even try that version of events. It all came down to his character and motivations.

Which, come to think of it, sounded a lot like every officer evaluation report he'd ever gotten. Nobody cared about what you did, just whether your rater used terms like 'stellar' and 'exemplary' or 'adequate' and 'unremarkable.'

On the witness stand, COL Patton once again painted a picture of Sam as unhinged and unreliable even before the alleged attempted homicide. Pretentious jerk. He was probably going through PowerPoint withdrawals after being stuck in court all day.

Then Dr. Smallwood gave his official findings. He was brief and brutal. Sam was a danger to himself and all around him. The doc recommended that Sam receive intensive in-patient care for the foreseeable future. His demonic shadow smirked at Sam throughout cross-examination.

Hello, padded cell.

Sam's lawyer—a young captain just out of law school—did her best to counter the prosecution's grim picture of Sam. Her first character witness was a former commander whom Sam had worked well with. He had good things to say but wasn't particularly eloquent.

Then LTC Karmi Diaz took the stand. She radiated confidence in her dress uniform, shoes making a precise *click click* as she crossed the courtroom. When she spoke, it was with authority, passion, and conviction. LTC Samuel Davidson was a sterling officer who'd suffered a tragic mental break following a career of wartime service. The alleged crime was the Army's fault, not Sam's. He was the example that other officers should strive to meet.

Her responses were long and riveting, a series of monologues about the virtues of the misunderstood staff officer struggling against the incompetent machine that was Army bureaucracy. Partway through, Sam started to wish he'd been recording her speech. It was epic, erudite, and ended with the clear conclusion that Sam was the victim, a good officer being destroyed by the very system he'd fought to uphold for nineteen years.

Sam straightened in his seat, her words stiffening his spine. If she believed that strongly in him, why shouldn't he believe in himself?

Then she was done, both lawyers gave closing statements, and it was all over but the verdict.

"All rise," said the bailiff. The room shuffled to its feet with a scraping of chairs. Behind the defendant's table, Sam stood stiffly to attention.

The sour-faced judge eyed Sam over his glasses. "On the charge of attempted homicide, I find the defendant … guilty."

Sam's knees tried to give out.

"You will be dishonorably discharged and stripped of all retirement benefits."

No surprise there. And he'd been so close to his pension.

Not that a retirement check mattered in prison. What would he buy? A new toothbrush? Sam met the judge's pinched gaze, waiting for the hammer to drop.

"As for confinement, the prosecution requested twenty years."

Sam's throat locked up.

"However, in consideration of the testimony received, I'm reducing that to time served and adding mandatory outpatient psychiatric care for five years." The gavel slammed down. "Court dismissed."

Sam's knees finally buckled. He dropped into his chair in shock. Hands clapped his shoulders. Voices clamored in his ears, but he didn't hear them. He was out of the Army with nothing to show for his nineteen years of service. But at least he wasn't going to prison. He was dimly aware of the bailiff removing his ankle monitor.

A voice that conjured images of mating weasels broke into his thoughts. "Samuel A. Davidson?"

Sam's head snapped up. He knew that voice.

The demon from Iraq, all two feet of him, stood in front of Sam in the same rumpled suit as before. This time Sam noticed that he didn't have shoes. His clawed feet were almost vulture-like. "I thought that was you," the imp said.

Sam's hindbrain once again tried to wrest control of his motor functions, but he didn't let it. Instead, he rose, ignoring the demon. Sam shook his lawyer's hand, thanked her profusely, then shook the hands of well-wishers—officers and NCOs who'd worked with him in the past. As soon as he could, Sam broke free and strode from the courtroom. The demon scrambled to keep up.

"The name's Alvin Bureaucracy," the balding little monster said. "Pursuant to official orders from Hell's Bureaucracy—yeah, it's the family name—I've been assigned as your personal tormentor. Congratulations!"

"My personal ... what?" Sam said, stopping dead in the marbled hall outside the courtroom.

"It's like a guardian angel, but in reverse. My job is to make your life a living hell, and I'm very good at my job." The demon grinned, showing entirely too many sharp teeth.

Karmi walked up with a concerned expression. She'd seen him talking to a demon that nobody else saw. Ignoring the little eel, Sam grabbed her hand and shook it hard enough to rattle her shoulder. "Karmi, I can't thank you enough for your help."

"Don't worry about it. I wouldn't be standing here if others hadn't done the same for me. Someday you'll meet someone who needs help only you can give. Help them without reservation."

"Definitely," Sam said, releasing her hand. Karmi glanced pointedly at the demon she couldn't see.

"Are you okay?"

Sam drew a deep breath and nodded. "I'm going to be. Thank you again."

With a warm smile and a nod, she turned and left.

Sam glanced back down at Alvin. What was he going to do about his personally assigned tormentor? The demon looked like he was already plotting some evil scheme to make Sam's life miserable.

Screw that.

Sam had managed to escape one bureaucratic system—with help, he was quick to remind himself—he could outwit another one. Sure, the Army had tossed him out like last night's garbage, but Sam was free. Eventually, he'd find a way to be free of Alvin's torments as well.

"So," he said to the demon, turning for the exit, "tell me about this 'Hell's Bureaucracy.' They have a lot of red tape?"

"Like you wouldn't believe!" Alvin said. "Just to get assigned to you, I had to submit seventeen requests to a dozen different offices, each of which required someone else's signature before they'd approve it. Why do you think it took me three months to come back?"

Sam nodded thoughtfully and pushed through the exit. War was hell, but that was behind him now. He had a new kind of hell—or rather, Hell—to wrangle as a civilian. But the more Alvin chattered, the more Sam relaxed. All bureaucracies were the same, be they earthly or infernal. He just had to learn the rules that governed this Hell's Bureaucracy—and then break them.

Then he would be free.

HELL'S BUREAUCRACY

"The saboteur should be ingenious in using his everyday equipment. All sorts of weapons will present themselves if he looks at his surroundings in a different light."
            – *The Simple Sabotage Field Manual*

Knowledge wasn't power, it was a curse.

Sam knew he hadn't misfiled anything, let alone the Waters account Form-5, but here he was, once again, taking the blame. He rocked back on his heels under Mr. Langowski's tirade, wishing he could explain everything.

Yes, sir. I did confirm receipt with accounting. Especially after last time.

No, files aren't in the habit of walking away. This one had help.

As a matter of fact, I do know who helped it walk away. It was the thieving little demon sitting on the cubicle wall right behind you.

They'd toss him in the loony bin!

Alvin, the two-foot-tall miscreant that only Sam saw, cackled from his perch as the boss's tirade escalated. Spittle hit Sam's cheek, and he flinched.

What a way to start the week.

Langowski finally left, and Sam collapsed into his chair and glared at Alvin. What he wouldn't give to escape the little hellion's torments. The demon looked pleased with himself and straightened his rumpled gray suit. Scrawny horns poked through his greasy comb-over, and his sharp red eyes twinkled.

"So, how was your weekend?" Alvin's voice sounded like a strangled weasel.

"Fine. Should have known you'd put in overtime just to make my Monday morning special." Sam kept his voice low.

Alvin grinned. Even demons like getting credit for a job well done. "I foresee a new policy coming. Form-5s in quadruplicate!" Sam groaned. The Form-5 was Alvin's invention. The little imp had turned Bridewell Incorporated into his personal bureaucratic playground, implementing crazy policies that everyone accepted. People don't question bureaucracy, they just complain about it. Sam sold corporate office supplies for Bridewell, which sucked, but he didn't have any better options. He'd been sacked twice because of Alvin.

The phone rang and Sam answered. He listened to the shrill voice at the other end, saying "uh-huh" and "okay" as appropriate before hanging up. He eyed Alvin. "Why are there two pallets of neon pink copy paper downstairs with my name on the order slip?"

Alvin's smile broadened, and Sam rolled his eyes. He'd expected more physical torment from his personally assigned demon—hot pincers, haunted dreams, that sort of thing—but Alvin's torments were more insidious. Bureaucratic.

Sam drummed his fingers on the desk. Two pallets of pink paper. Langowski would blow a gasket. He heaved himself up and headed for the elevator.

The loading dock smelled of diesel fumes despite the open bay door that let in chill January winds. Alvin scurried away as Sam headed toward the receiving desk, and he breathed a sigh of relief. Good riddance.

A portly truck driver stepped from behind the double-stacked pallets of paper and Sam froze. It wasn't the driver who struck him speechless, but the hulking angel standing *behind* the man, a claymore on his back. The angel's bushy blonde eyebrows rose when he realized Sam could see him.

Sam had never seen an angel before. He'd asked Alvin about the paucity of spirits in the world and received a snarky remark about mankind breeding like rabbits. Too many people, not enough spirits to manage them.

The driver ignored Sam's expression, handed him the manifest for signature, then waddled off toward the restroom. His guardian angel didn't follow.

The receiving clerk's shrill voice drew Sam's attention. "Where's this going?" She waved at the pallets.

"Joe Harridan in Marketing." He and Joe had a good-natured feud and this was just the thing to ratchet it up a notch.

"Fine," the clerk said, looking sour. "But you're filling out the Form-5."

Sam grimaced, but nodded. The angel turned and marched through the bay door. Sam followed, trying to look nonchalant. Snow crunched underfoot. Sam folded his arms against winter's chill.

"You have a demon problem," the angel said in a voice that rumbled like thunder.

"Wow, that's direct. What happened to 'Oh my, you can see me?'"

"God works in mysterious ways."

Sam opened his mouth for another sarcastic retort, but the angel's lofty expression made him close it again. He already had a demon problem. Best not to add an angel problem, too.

The angel inclined his head. "I am Tobias. How did you acquire your demon?"

"Nicked myself on an ancient ceremonial dagger when I was still in the Army. I was helping catalog Iraqi artifacts when it happened. My third eye opened, I saw the little twit tormenting a major, and I freaked out. Drew my weapon and, well, things went downhill from there. Alvin got excited when he realized I could see him, then disappeared. By the time the court-marshal ended, he'd returned claiming he'd been assigned as my personal demon. Like a guardian angel, but in reverse. Any suggestions for getting rid of him?"

"Banish him to Hell with a blessed blade. He shan't return."

"Don't have one of those. Could *you* banish him?"

"My duties lie elsewhere. Were you of the faithful, I would offer a permanent solution involving prayer and supplication. However, I sense little faith within you."

Sam snorted. "Faith is the belief in things unseen. I see this little prat torment me every day. I'm more of a realist."

Tobias gazed skyward, then rumbled a sigh. "I can bless your blade if you have one at hand."

Sam *didn't* have one at hand but pursed his lips as an idea hit him. Making Tobias promise to wait, he dashed inside, snatched an empty folder from the receiving desk, and headed upstairs. He stepped onto the fifth floor at a brisk walk, head down, folder in hand. He'd discovered in the Army that a folder and a brisk pace were a magic shield against idle chit-chat and additional work. Everyone assumed you were doing Something Important and left you alone.

"Sam!" Langowski yelled, spying him from across the room.

Everyone, that is, except the boss. But even he could be fooled by the folder.

Sam waived his manila shield. "Working on it, sir!" Langowski's door slammed shut, and Sam grinned. At his desk, he grabbed his blade—a six-inch medieval sword letter opener he'd bought on a layover in Germany. He used it to add that necessary barbarism when opening official correspondence. One more masterful Hard Working Employee impression and Sam was back in the elevator.

In the loading bay, the driver had his truck's hood up, complaining about a temperamental starter. Sam eyed the angelic claymore thrust into the engine block but refrained from comment and headed outside.

Tobias raised an eyebrow when Sam presented his letter opener. It must have passed muster because the angel laid hands upon it and prayed in Latin. Sam's miniature broadsword glowed brightly before returning to normal.

Tobias placed a weightless hand on Sam's shoulder, sending peace and tranquility through him. "May God bless you on your quest and bring you a little faith." Sam wasn't sure about that last part, but Heaven had just granted him a solution to his demon problem. He wasn't about to quibble.

Sam managed a solemn, "Thank you," before Tobias returned to the truck, withdrew his claymore, and slid into the passenger seat. The driver climbed in beside his unseen passenger and tried the starter once more.

The claymore-free engine roared to life. Sam waved goodbye, and headed inside to slay his demon.

***

Demon slaying in corporate America was more difficult than Sam expected. His tormentor seemed to have disappeared. By the end of the day, Sam's patience had run out. He tucked Faith—which seemed a fitting name for his blessed letter opener—into his suit jacket and went demon hunting. Sam searched three floors before he found Alvin sauntering out of the legal office, whistling a jaunty tune.

That wasn't good.

No matter. It was time to end this. Sam's eyes narrowed, and his pulse raced. The hallway was empty.

He drew Faith and slashed. Alvin screeched and jumped back, clawed hands raised. Faith sliced his palm, releasing something black and gaseous.

"Hey, what's the big idea?" Alvin squawked, then glanced at his palm. "You got a blessed blade?! Oh, shi—"

With a *pop*, Alvin disappeared and Sam was free.

***

Sam rolled into work the next morning whistling Alvin's jaunty tune, his heart light. His whistle trailed off when he found Alvin sitting on his desk, arms crossed, red eyes furious.

"I thought I banished you," Sam said, his throat tight.

"You did." Alvin rose, fists clenched. "HR was ... displeased."

"HR ... on the first floor?"

"*Hell's Resources,* asshole. I'm getting audited because of you."

"But you were *banished.* How'd you get back?"

"Please." Alvin rolled his eyes. "Bureaucracy is my family name. We invented red tape. You think I couldn't short-list myself for a return trip?"

Shit.

Panic blanked Sam's mind. He drew Faith and lunged. Alvin dodged and scrambled over the cubicle wall. Sam had one hand on the wall and a knee on his desk when the elevator dinged, and Langowski stepped out.

"Sam! What the *hell* were you thinking filing a breach of contract against Waters? We just got that account!"

What?

Sam straightened and scowled, remembering Alvin's

trip to legal. The little fiend! He sheathed Faith inside his jacket and trailed into Langowski's office. As the door closed behind him, he glanced back.

Alvin was perched atop the cubicle wall, fire in his eyes. He pointed a clawed finger. "I will destroy you."

The door clicked shut.

***

Between the Waters debacle and Alvin's tedious torments, Sam barely survived the week. Langowski threatened to fire him but clearly enjoyed having a verbal punching bag around. Sam kept trying to banish Alvin, but the slippery eel evaded him. By Friday, Sam despaired of catching the little beast. Besides, what was the point? He'd just bounce right back the next day.

Sam was stewing at his desk when a sharp New York accent made him glance up.

"Two pallets of pink paper? Good one, Sam."

Joe Harridan, Sam's rival from Marketing, grinned over the cubicle wall. Joe was tall, muscled, and a favorite among the ladies. Everything Sam wasn't. Sam leaned back and switched mental gears.

"Thought you'd like the challenge."

"I saw you coming a mile away." Joe pinned a pink flyer to the cubicle wall with his fingers. "Langowski just approved our Valentine's Day ad campaign. These babies go out this afternoon."

Sam scanned the pink trifold's beautiful display of Bridewell's office supplies. *Free shipping for the first hundred orders. Call now!* Sam's phone number was printed in large text at the bottom.

"You bastard," he said, admiring the subtlety. He'd have to man his phone all weekend or the campaign would flounder—and Sam would get blamed. It was a slick move, the kind Alvin might think up. Sam glanced around and spied the demon typing away in an unoccupied cubicle across the aisle.

"Takes one to know one," Joe replied cheerily and swaggered away. "I look forward to reading the results in your report. Good luck!"

Oh, yeah. Reports were due. Of all the screwed-up policies Alvin had implemented at Bridewell, the individual weekly reports were particularly insidious—an information overload that supervisors never read, preferring to invent their own lies. It hadn't taken long for Bridewell's employees to turn the reports into a game of creative exaggeration. Sam and Joe were the current battling champions.

Sam eyed Alvin, struck by the demon's intense focus. What was he doing? Sam tip-toed over then froze when he saw the screen. Alvin was typing a report to his superiors in Hell—on a Bridewell computer. Sam frowned. The company network was connected to the Underworld? That explained a lot about the IT department.

Sam slipped back to his desk and opened the share drive. He scanned folders, lips pursed, unsure what he was looking for.

Odd. There was a folder labeled Human Resources and another labeled HR.

Hell's Resources?

Sam clicked and received a password request. He leaned back and pondered, fingers drumming the desk. Then he rocked forward, typed "Bureaucracy," and hit enter.

Bingo. Humans aren't the only ones with lazy passwords.

It contained a single folder titled Samuel Davidson Project which held five years of Alvin's reports. Unlike the rest of the share drive, these were neatly organized and—according to the metadata—unopened since Alvin wrote them. His boss never read his reports.

More importantly, Alvin's audit hadn't begun yet. It'd be a shame if those files disappeared.

A maniacal cackle built inside Sam's chest.

Select all. Shift-delete. Why yes, I *do* want to permanently delete all...

No. Not permanently. That was too cruel. Besides, a career of dealing with vindictive bureaucrats had ingrained the importance of keeping copies of *everything*. But he had to do something.

With a quick drag-and-drop, Sam moved the reports to his desktop.

A shriek erupted from across the aisle. "No-no-NO!" Sam spun his chair and watched with wicked glee as Alvin bolted for the elevator. Within seconds, the floor indicator descended to the basement, home of the IT department.

Nice try.

Sam disconnected his computer's network cable with a satisfied sigh. No demonic help desk would find those files now. Freedom was so close.

The office emptied out early, but Sam didn't leave. He'd attracted too much attention to skate out before the boss. He idly read Alvin's reports—such elegant malarkey—until Langowski finally left, taking the stairs.

The elevator slid open and Alvin stepped out, shoulders slumped. The file recovery had clearly failed. The little wretch climbed into his borrowed cubicle's chair and spun around slowly.

A pang of guilt wormed its way into Sam's heart. Perhaps he'd gone too far. But Alvin was a demon. Shouldn't the rules be different?

Sam eyed the clock and shelved the feeling for a moment. He had another problem that needed attention—Joe's pretty pink ad campaign. Sam dialed call-forwarding on his office phone then entered Joe's mobile number. Hopeful customers would start bombarding his rival's phone first thing tomorrow morning. Sam chuckled.

Your move, Joe.

The elevator dinged open, and Sam glanced up. His breath caught at the over-tall demon who ducked through the doors. Sam dropped behind his cubicle wall and peered into the aisle.

The demon was impossibly gaunt, like a stick figure drawn on silly-putty then stretched until his horns brushed the ceiling. He wore a rumpled suit that matched Alvin's and gold-wire spectacles framed his red eyes. Clawed fingers drummed on an oversized clipboard as he scanned the room.

The Auditor had arrived.

The demon lumbered to Alvin's cubicle and spoke with a voice as dry as crumpled ash. "Alvin Bureaucracy?"

Alvin climbed onto the desk and stood eye-to-chest with the lanky demon. "Yes, *Auditor*?" he sneered. Nobody likes auditors.

"Your audit begins now. Should—*when*—you fail, you will be assigned a torment-coach from the Office of Micromanagement for on-the-job training."

Woah. The Office of Micromanagement? And Sam thought human bureaucracy was nasty. Plus, "on-the-job training" didn't sound promising for Sam's demon-free life.

The Auditor droned on. "In the improbable event that you pass, you will receive the promotion you were due"—he consulted his clipboard—"fifty-seven years ago."

Sam stifled a gasp. That was it. Alvin's overdue promotion was his ticket to freedom.

Parchment rustled as the Auditor flipped a page. "Bring up your reports."

Alvin stammered, but Sam popped up like a jack-in-a-box. "Found 'em!" The Auditor spun and blinked at Sam, who gave his most charming smile. "IT must have moved some folders around," he lied and waved at his screen. Alvin eyed Sam dubiously, but stalked over and clambered into his chair. The demon sagged in relief when he saw the reports.

The Auditor gaped at Sam. "You ... can see us? Oh, my." He flipped through his clipboard. "There's nothing about that in my files."

Sam smirked. That's what happens when supervisors don't read reports. "Yup, and I'm glad I can. I couldn't ask for a better tormentor than Alvin."

"Really?" both demons said in unison.

"I've learned a lot from this little rascal. He's been making my life a living hell for five years!" No lie there. "Just today I used one of his tricks to ruin my coworker's weekend."

The Auditor's gaze swung toward Alvin, brows furrowed. "Your charge spreads torments on your behalf?"

"That's right." Alvin puffed out his chest, quick to take

credit where none was due. "Pitting humans against each other is the epitome of evil."

"Indeed." The Auditor huffed. "This is most irregular." He adjusted his glasses and scanned his checklist. "Hmm. About those reports…"

Sam stepped back as Alvin sailed through his audit, the Auditor bent double to see Sam's screen. He fingered Faith and contemplated banishing them both, but decided against it. Banishment was temporary. This plan would free him forever. It had to.

Finally, the Auditor rose to his full imposing height.

"So, how'd he do?" Sam asked brightly.

"I am … surprised." The Auditor sighed like crackling embers. "Nobody passes my audits, but Alvin Bureaucracy's files were impeccable." He made a final checkmark and glared at his clipboard as though searching for an error.

Sam wasn't surprised. He'd never met a nastier, more capable bureaucrat than Alvin.

The Auditor tucked his clipboard under an elbow and looked at Sam's tormentor. "I will file the Form-5 with HR for your promotion and reassignment." With another disappointed sigh, the lanky demon lumbered toward the elevator. Eyes bright, Alvin leapt from Sam's chair to follow.

Sam waved. "Good luck on the next assignment!" It had worked. In the name of all that was holy...

The Auditor's clawed hand slapped the closing elevator doors, stopping them. Evil red eyes bored into Sam's. "I have noted you in my report, Samuel Davidson. Expect your replacement tormentor shortly."

Sam's jaw dropped and the door slid shut with a cheerful *ding*.

***

No tormentor arrived over the weekend, so Sam wondered if he'd misheard the Auditor. It was too much to hope for, but hope and Faith were all he had. Driving to work on Monday, his hand kept drifting toward the blessed blade in his jacket.

He parked in the underground garage and plodded toward the elevators. He'd almost reached them when a gravelly voice behind him asked, "Samuel Davidson?"

Sam jumped and spun. A demon with long tusks and no sense of personal space fiddled with the buttons of his wrinkled suit. "Who's asking?" Sam's hand slipped inside his jacket.

A toothy grin spread across a face that even a mother couldn't love. "Brutus Bureaucracy, your new tormentor. I would have been here Saturday, but HR lost my paperwork. Twice." First-day nerves were obvious in Brutus's rushed speech. "My cousin Alvin assigned me—he's head of Bureaucratic Torments now—and, well, I'm so excited for this opportunity to make your life a living hell."

Sam's jaw clenched. No. Not again. He whipped out Faith and stabbed Brutus Bureaucracy in the shoulder. The demon looked at the blade in surprise before disappearing with a *pop*.

***

Clarissa Bureaucracy arrived the next day, a hulking horned gorilla who caught Sam outside the restroom. He hadn't slept well and overcompensated with coffee, so his bladder was ready to burst. He didn't have time for niceties. Sam banished the cheerful Clarissa before she even finished her introduction.

Desmond Bureaucracy was more cautious when he arrived on Wednesday. He approached Sam's cubicle while a coworker bent his ear about her grandson's adorable puke—complete with pictures. Sam was contemplating the comparative joys of a root canal when his new tormentor caught his eye. Desmond introduced himself over the old woman's prattling before skittering away.

Clever. Sam couldn't stab the demon with a coworker watching. Swinging a sword around the office, even a miniature one, was frowned upon in corporate America. Still, Sam cornered Desmond the next day and banished him as he pilfered a Form-5 on its way to accounting.

The following week Sam banished Eugene, Francisco, and Gloria Bureaucracy. None were around long enough to provide more than annoyance-level torments, but this was getting old.

He arrived early on Friday and found Alvin sitting on his keyboard, arms crossed. His old nemesis looked pissed.

"You have to stop banishing my cousins. The Auditor is crucifying us!"

Sam hoped he was being figurative. "Stop sending them. You're the head of Bureaucratic Torments now. You can end this."

Alvin ran clawed fingers through his comb-over. "I can't. You impressed the Auditor and caught the attention of HR. Everyone wants to torment you!"

Sam fought the urge to banish the little twit and leaned against his cubicle, arms crossed. "So, I'm doomed to eternal torment because I helped you?"

"Well, living torment. The state of your eternal soul is still in question."

That made Sam pause, but he wasn't prepared to debate theology with a demon. He glared. There was only one way out.

It was time to make a deal with the devil.

"I don't have to banish your cousins," Sam said, and Alvin perked up. "Could you assign another cousin to me and then redirect them without Hell's Resources noticing?"

"I *am* the master of misdirected paperwork." Alvin's nasal tone was both cocky and cautious.

"Good. I don't care where they go so long as I don't see them. They can drink mimosas in Tahiti for all I care. I'll write their reports, giving every appearance of creatively perpetual torment, while you set up a rotating vacation schedule for your favored cousins."

"Won't work. Demons from outside the family have already elbowed their way into the Department of Bureaucratic Torments. They'll notice."

"Okay. Make the interlopers supervisors. Send them up here to check on your cousins, and I'll banish them back to Hell. That will reinforce your need for resources while removing troublemakers from your ranks." The little devil's eyes sparkled as the idea took hold. "You'll expand your empire, protect the family name, and get credit for tormenting me, while I"—Sam drew Faith and brandished it at Alvin—"will be free from you. Forever."

Alvin blanched at the blessed blade before Sam returned Faith to his pocket and asked, "So, do we have a deal?"

***

The devil is in the details. Alvin should have paid closer attention when Sam sold his time instead of his soul. Sam carefully noted when the little cretin stopped reading his reports, then employed the digital form of his manila shield trick—with an added twist. He maintained his Hard Working Employee ruse, ensuring that files appeared exactly on schedule, but completely changed the tenor of their content.

He told the truth.

The reports became a confession of their deal—complete with a running tally of the demons banished on Alvin's behalf. Sam signed them "Demon Slayer" and each report reached a single, inescapable conclusion.

Tormenting Samuel Davidson was not in Hell's best interests.

Hell's Resources would eventually notice the rising number of banishments and stop sending demons. Then Sam would be free. Until then, he would hunt demons and write his reports. He'd learned how to fight Hell's Bureaucracy—from the inside and with proper documentation—and reveled in the challenge.

Knowledge wasn't a curse. It was power.

LEMON GRENADES

"Create a situation in which the citizen-saboteur acquires a sense of responsibility and begins to educate others in simple sabotage."

– The Simple Sabotage Field Manual

Sam picked up the lemon grenade sitting on his desk. It was one of those plastic squeezy lemons, but instead of a standard flip top for adding a dash of juice to your drink, it had a blue-spooned training grenade fuze jammed into it. An aged strip of green Army-style duct tape around the neck held the Frankenstein-of-fake-fruits together. Time and handling had paled the plastic lemon, but it was still supple, as if a simple squeeze would add a dash of lemon-flavored TNT to Sam's morning coffee.

Not a flavor he wanted to try, to be honest.

"Sam," Inez said from his office doorway. "We need to go. Lazarus is feeling a bit impatient. Analisa's breakthrough for Immortus actually has him excited for once." Sam's wife ran her fingers through her short red hair, clearly anxious to get moving.

Today was a big day for the company, a possible breakthrough after literal millennia of planning and research into the nature of the human soul, yet Sam couldn't find it in himself to be as excited as everyone else. They had officially been part of Immortus Inc. for only a short time, and it had sounded great when they got their job offers—he as Chief of Logistics Support, Inez as Chief of Public Relations. He and Inez had known about the project for years—her much longer than he—but hadn't joined up until Lazarus himself dropped by to recruit them. Yes, *that* Lazarus. When an immortal personally asks for your help, you think twice before saying no.

The shine hadn't taken long to wear off. Immortus was just another corporation, though one whose existence had remained hidden for centuries under layers of shell companies and high-paid lawyers. Only in the past decade had they come into the open, building their hundred-acre campus in the middle of nowhere Iowa.

Sam had to admit that Immortus started with an incredible vision: immortality on Earth for everyone. Lazarus was—is—one of only thirteen immortals in the entire world. He'd accomplished great things in the past two thousand years. Given equal opportunity, why couldn't others do the same?

It sounded good, it really did, but somewhere over the last few centuries, Immortus lost its way. Corruption, greed, and bureaucratic bloat became the name of the day. Research required funding and funding came with strings. At this point, if they did achieve immortality, only the obscenely rich would benefit from it.

As the first white-collar son of a blue-collar family, that idea didn't sit well with Sam.

He smiled at Inez but didn't rise. "You go ahead, honey, I'll be there in a minute."

She cocked an eyebrow but didn't argue. Inez knew Sam well enough to know that he'd tell her what was bothering him. Eventually.

Inez was a true believer in the Immortus vision. But why wouldn't she be? She was one of the thirteen immortals. She loved Sam as much as he loved her, the missing half of his soul whom he'd literally gone to Hell and back with. To her, Immortus would be Sam's salvation when the Reaper came calling. After millennia alone, she'd taken a chance on love and didn't want to let him go after a mere single lifetime.

Sam was all about avoiding Grim's blade. But he wasn't so sure that Immortus was the answer.

Inez crossed the well-appointed office to Sam's desk and leaned down for a quick kiss. "Don't take too long. You know Laz will note your absence." He nodded and then she was gone.

As the door closed, Sam leaned his elbows on his desk, contemplating the lemon grenade in his hands. He'd had a lot of desks over the years, some big, some small, and one in the comfort of his basement during a glorious yet brief stint of teleworking. Yet no matter how often the desk changed, that lemon grenade remained the same: a reminder that there is always a better way. Today, of all days, he needed that reminder.

Sam would never forget the day that lemon grenade entered his life—at high velocity on its terminal arc toward his head, thrown by the delightfully deranged Sergeant Rosati. Well, perhaps 'delightfully deranged' wasn't a fair description of SGT Rosati. He was smart and witty, a chain-smoking Army pharmacist turned ammunition handler, a job change that definitely was not his decision. But those are the dangers of working for one of the biggest bureaucracies in the world. You take what you're given, or you go home with your tail between your legs. With thinning hair, pockmarked skin, and the figure of an anorexic goose, SGT Rosati looked like he'd been literally put through the wringer to squeeze every ounce of joy from his soul. His smile always had an edge to it. He was by far the most disgruntled NCO Sam had ever met, which was saying a lot.

Life had given Rosati a *lot* of lemons.

Sam met SGT Rosati back when he was a lieutenant in the United States Army. The gangly sergeant was the company training NCO who coordinated unit training events and records (because without records, the training never happened and you have to do it all over again ... yay, Army). It was a thankless job, and SGT Rosati was good at it. He was good at it because he knew how the system worked, how to work the system, and when to break the system for its own good.

Soldiers had a saying: there's a right way, a wrong way, and the Army way of doing things. Somehow, SGT Rosati had added 'the Rosati way of doing things' to that list in Sam's mind.

The Army way typically involved extra steps, duplicated efforts, and (of course) proper documentation that the task was completed. Take, for example, the simple task of showing up for work.

Outside the Army, arriving bright-eyed and bushy-tailed with an extra cup of joe for your favorite coworker might be considered the right way of showing up for work. Dragging yourself through the door ten minutes late still buzzed from the bar and reeking of booze and cigarettes? That could be considered the wrong way. But hey, you showed up, right? Task complete, only a thousand more until it's time to clock out.

There's a world of possibility between those two extremes, but the concept remains simple. There's a right way and a wrong way. The Army way, however, was neither better nor worse than these extremes. It was more ... bureaucratic.

First formation was always at six thirty in the morning. Reveille would sound, everyone saluted, and the day began. But you couldn't roll up to formation just as the bugle sounded. Oh, no. That's not the Army way. To ensure everybody arrived on time, the first sergeant held a pre-formation ten minutes prior to actual formation. Because, to quote that bastion of military propriety, "If you're early, you're on time. If you're on time, you're late. And if you're late ... you'd better be in the hospital or dead."

Yeah, the Army had some great sayings. But hey, what's ten extra minutes? Sounds reasonable.

And that's how bureaucracy gets you. Everything sounds reasonable until it isn't.

The platoon sergeant added another ten minutes to his soldiers' arrival because he wanted to ensure that *his* platoon was on time for the first sergeant. Then the squad leader added *another* ten minutes because he was tired of getting yelled at by the platoon sergeant every time Private Joe Snuffy rolled up less than twenty minutes early. Suddenly, everyone was in formation a full thirty minutes before absolutely necessary ... and everyone thought this was normal. They'd just stand around in the dark, in the cold, waiting for someone to push a button so a canned bugle call would sound over the loudspeaker.

Every. Single. Day. Heaven help them if there was a Brigade or Division run. Sam remembered arriving a full hour before a division run and shivering in the sleeting snow just so the leadership could ensure everyone was lined up pretty before Reveille sounded.

Sure, everyone complained about it, but a soldier wasn't happy unless they had something to complain about. Nobody ever tried to change anything or buck the Army way.

Except for SGT Rosati.

One day, Sam popped into the training office for a chat with the chain-smoking sergeant about some upcoming training event. Sam never caught him smoking inside, but Rosati always smelled like he'd just taken a long puff off a menthol. The nicotine in his office was so thick that Sam could taste it. As he pushed the door open, he raised an inquiring finger to get the emaciated sergeant's attention and—

"Frag out!" SGT Rosati yelled. A lemon hurtled toward Sam's head with the distinctive sound of a grenade's spring-loaded spoon flying free.

Sam panicked. He'd never been good at sports that involved small objects flying toward his face. He always avoided softball and baseball as a kid, preferring soccer because at least the ball stayed on the ground and was big enough to (usually) avoid when it flew toward his face at Mach Three.

Sam ducked, screamed a battle cry that maaaay have sounded like a kid finding a spider, and swung his open palm at the incoming grenade.

His hand connected with a *thwap!* The lemon hurtled back toward his attacker. SGT Rosati caught it with a grin and rose from behind his desk. "Nicely done, LT," he said, an unlit cigarette dangling from his lips.

Sam's breath came hard and fast. "What the hell?!"

SGT Rosati retrieved the grenade spoon from the floor and reattached it to his unexploded lemon. Upon closer examination, Sam saw that it wasn't an actual lemon, but one of those plastic ones from the grocery store. Jammed into it and attached with green tape was an expended training grenade fuze (harmless, but it still looked real). SGT Rosati slipped the pin back into the grenade and presented it to Sam with these fateful words:

"When life gives you lemons, make lemon grenades."

Sam blinked at him. "What about making lemonade?" he asked and dubiously examined his prize.

SGT Rosati pulled the unlit cigarette from his lips and examined it as though it contained the secrets to life, the universe, and everything. Finally, he said, "Life's gonna give you a lot of lemons, LT. Making lemonade is all well and good, a way to make the best of a bad situation. But when life gives me problems, I prefer to fight back. Thus"—he tapped the little plastic lemon with his cigarette—"lemon grenades."

Sam held the lemon up, turning it for a proper examination. Now that his initial shock was over, he had to admit that he wasn't surprised by SGT Rosati's perspective. The Army had ground him up and spit him back out. They'd even taken his rank a couple of times through no fault of his own. Apparently, there was some obscure regulatory caveat about enlisted soldiers losing a rank when they transferred between Active Army to the Reserves and back again. Yet, despite the setbacks, SGT Rosati had done more than just survive in the bureaucracy. He'd thrived. He was the guy who could get everything and could get *away* with anything. He could even roll up to formation as the bugle blared without the first sergeant even batting an eye.

"How do you do it?" Sam asked.

SGT Rosati's scraggly eyebrow rose. "It's just a fuze taped to a plastic lemon, LT. I think even you could figure that out."

"No," Sam said. "I mean, how do you take all the lemons

the Army chucks your way and come back swinging for the home run? The system keeps trying to break you, but you're still here."

The sergeant considered this, sucking the end of his unlit cigarette. "The Army's not malicious, it's not kind, it just is. It's a machine too big for any single individual to steer. If you fight the bureaucracy head-on, you'll lose every time. I know, I've tried. Stay in the bureaucracy long enough and you'll either become part of the problem, or you'll end up broken and discarded. Most career soldiers become part of the problem. Assimilation is easier than resistance."

"Where do the lemon grenades come in?"

SGT Rosati grinned. "You know the theory of lemon cars?"

"Sure. Cars made on a Monday when nobody wants to come to work tend to be poorly assembled."

"People are the same way. Some folks in the Army come out bright and shiny like the rank on your collar. They're the true believers ready to defend the Army way against all comers. Others get spat out of the system like me: gnarled and twisted and willing to bend a few rules to make life livable for myself and those around me. Folk like me tend to survive by finding each other." He rolled the cigarette from one side of his lips to the other with his tongue and nodded to the plastic lemon in Sam's hand. "With a lemon car, you'd return it to the weasel of a salesman who sold it to you in hopes of something better coming out of the deal. Lemon grenades are the same. They aren't about creating glorious chaos—though that can be fun. They're about exploiting weaknesses in the system. When someone gives you a sour problem, LT, figure out how to chuck it back at them so the mess ends up in their lap, not yours."

***

It had been decades since Sam had seen SGT Rosati, though he often thought about him when bureaucracy reared its ugly head. Life outside the military was different, but bureaucracies were the same everywhere. Sure, Immortus Incorporated was smaller than the U.S. Army, but it had been around much longer.

Sam had been disappointed by what he found under the glitter of Immortus's seemingly endless budget. Just like the Army, there was a right way, a wrong way, and an Immortus way. And the Immortus was less concerned with morals than profit.

Hooray for corporate greed.

They'd made amazing medical breakthroughs, but Sam couldn't help thinking about who would benefit and who would ultimately suffer once they cracked the code. Who would become the first generation of immortals? Sam could guarantee it wouldn't be people like SGT Rosati.

A clearing throat brought Sam back to the present. He glanced at the door and was surprised to see Lazarus himself filling the doorway. The immortal looked barely older than Sam, like a middle-aged businessman: clean-shaven with wavy brown hair, a hint of a tan, and a simple off-the-rack suit.

Sam's concerns must have shown on his face. Lazarus thrust his hands into his pockets and strode in. "What's wrong, Sam?"

He smiled at his immortal boss and rose. "Nothing. Sorry, I just got caught up reminiscing."

Lazarus nodded with understanding, his relaxed posture at odds with the tightness around his eyes. "Nothing wrong with that ... at the appropriate time." He nodded his head toward the hallway. "There are a lot of very important people waiting for us. Our backers flew in especially for Analisa's demonstration today. Shall we?" His tone was light, but the order was clear.

Our backers. The billionaires who were funding their own immortality. Once they had it, what would they do with their endless time? Make the world a better place because they were in it?

Not likely.

Something snapped inside Sam, some final bit of resistance. He couldn't let Immortus succeed. Lazarus may have the best intentions, but he'd dealt with the devil to achieve his ends and now there was something sick at the core of the company.

Yet, Sam couldn't stop Immortus on his own. SGT Rosati had warned against fighting the system head-on. It would crush him. The NCO's voice rose in Sam's memory. "Folk like me tend to survive by finding each other."

Sam wasn't alone in his doubts. He couldn't be. There had to be someone else ready to buck the system and stop Immortus. Sam just had to find them. That was the Rosati way.

He followed Lazarus out the door, the sergeant's words ringing in his mind.

Quietly, he pocketed the lemon grenade.

The End

Sam will return in Death and the Immortal, *the third installment of the Grimsworld series, coming in 2026.*

Author Note

The following pages contain excerpts from the *Simple Sabotage Field Manual* published by the Office of Strategic Services (Provisional) in 1944 and declassified by the Central Intelligence Agency in 2008. The full text can be found at CIA.gov or other websites that offer it for free download. There are even a few vendors selling copies on Amazon if you feel so inclined. The only changes from the original text are punctuation and formatting to fit this publication format and modern grammar expectations (i.e. motor-cycles is now motorcycles). I've added a handful of minor notes in parentheses and italics to add original definitions for words whose meaning may have drifted over time.

I also maaaay have added some parenthetical snark throughout. Alright, a lot of snark. Sorry, I couldn't help myself. In short, anything in parentheses and italics is entirely my interpretation of the regulation and didn't appear in the original text.

Also, remember that this original publication was from a time when gender pronouns in writing were primarily masculine, but know that this manual may be enjoyed by anyone regardless of gender up to and including androids, aliens (as in not from this Earth), werewolves, vampires, and zombies.

If you do find a zombie reading *Simple Sabotage*, I recommend backing away quietly before they get ideas. Zombies are not known for subtlety.

These excerpts from the *Simple Sabotage Field Manual* are provided purely for entertainment and to provide an interesting historical backdrop to the stories you just read. Enjoy.

Simple Sabotage
Field Manual

Strategic Services
(Provisional)

STRATEGIC SERVICE FIELD MANUAL No. 3

Washington, D.C.

17 January 1944

This Simple Sabotage Field Manual—Strategic Services (Provisional) is published for the information and guidance of all concerned and will be used as the basic doctrine for Strategic Services training on this subject.

The contents of this Manual should be carefully controlled and should not be allowed to come into unauthorized hands.

The instructions may be placed in separate pamphlets or leaflets according to categories of operations but should be distributed with care and not broadly. They should be used as a basis of radio broadcasts only for local and special cases and as directed by the theater commander.

AR 380-5, pertaining to the handling of secret documents, will be complied with in the handling of this Manual.

(Original signed)

William J. Donovan

CONTENTS

94

SIMPLE SABOTAGE

1. INTRODUCTION

a. The purpose of this paper is to characterize simple sabotage, to outline its possible effects, and to present suggestions for inciting and executing it.

b. Sabotage varies from highly technical *coup de main* (*sudden surprise attack as made by a military*) acts that require detailed planning and the use of specially trained operatives, to innumerable simple acts which the ordinary individual citizen-saboteur can perform. This paper is primarily concerned with the latter type. Simple sabotage does not require specially prepared tools or equipment; it is executed by an ordinary citizen who may or may not act individually and without the necessity for active connection with an organized group; and it is carried out in such a way as to involve a minimum danger of injury, detection, and reprisal.

c. Where destruction is involved, the weapons of the citizen-saboteur are salt, nails, candles, pebbles, thread, or any other materials he might normally be expected to possess as a householder or as a worker in his particular occupation (*or for a more modern context: pens, pencils, cor-*

rosive sodas, and the plastic silverware in your desk drawer). His arsenal is the kitchen shelf, the trash pile, his own usual kit of tools and supplies. The targets of his sabotage are usually objects to which he has normal and inconspicuous access in everyday life (*such as the sandwich your boss leaves in the community fridge every day*).

d. A second type of simple sabotage requires no destructive tools whatsoever and produces physical damage, if any, by highly indirect means. It is based on universal opportunities to make faulty decisions, to adopt a non-cooperative attitude, and to induce others to follow suit. Making a faulty decision may be simply a matter of placing tools in one spot instead of another. A non-cooperative attitude may involve nothing more than creating an unpleasant situation among one's fellow workers, engaging in bickerings, or displaying surliness and stupidity. (*I've known many coworkers who fit this description. I wonder if they read this manual or were naturally subversive.*)

e. This type of activity, sometimes referred to as the "human element," is frequently responsible for accidents, delays, and general obstruction even under normal conditions. (*Sounds like a definition of everyday life in a bureaucracy.*) The potential saboteur should discover what types of faulty decisions and non-cooperation are *normally* found in his kind of work and should then devise his sabotage so as to enlarge that "margin for error."

2. POSSIBLE EFFECTS

a. Acts of simple sabotage are occurring throughout Europe. An effort should be made to add to their efficiency, lessen their detectability, and increase their number. Acts of simple sabotage, multiplied by thousands of citizen-saboteurs, can be an effective weapon against the enemy. Slashing tires, draining fuel tanks, starting fires, starting arguments, acting stupidly, short-circuiting electric systems, and abrading machine parts will waste materials, manpower, and time. Occurring on a wide scale, simple sabotage will be a constant and tangible drag on the war effort of the enemy. (*On a bureaucratic scale, simply having an entire floor dependent on a single faulty printer and/or network server can bring the wheels of bureaucracy to a screeching halt. Ask me how I know.*)

b. Simple sabotage may also have secondary results of more or less value. Widespread practice of simple sabotage will harass and demoralize enemy administrators and police. Further, success may embolden the citizen-saboteur eventually to find colleagues who can assist him in sabotage of greater dimensions. Finally, the very practice of simple sabotage by natives in enemy or occupied territory may make these individuals identify themselves actively with the United Nations war effort, and encourage them to assist openly in periods of Allied invasion and occupation.

3. MOTIVATING THE SABOTEUR

a. To incite the citizen to active practice of simple sabotage and to keep him practicing that sabotage over sustained periods is a special problem. (*It takes a lot to make a career employee turn against the system. God help you when they do.*)

b. Simple sabotage is often an act which the citizen performs according to his own initiative and inclination. Acts of destruction do not bring him any personal gain and may be completely foreign to his habitually conservationist attitude toward materials and tools. Purposeful stupidity is contrary to human nature. (*This was clearly written in a time before social media. Ah, the good old days when stupidity wasn't normal.*) He frequently needs pressure, stimulation or assurance, and information and suggestions regarding feasible methods of simple sabotage.

(1) *Personal Motives*

(a) The ordinary citizen very probably has no immediate personal motive for committing simple sabotage. Instead, he must be made to anticipate indirect personal gain, such as might come with enemy evacuation or destruction of the ruling government group. Gains should be stated as specifically as possible for the area addressed: simple sabotage will hasten the day when Commissioner X and his deputies Y and Z will be thrown out, when particularly obnoxious decrees and restrictions will be abolished, when food will arrive, and so on. Abstract verbalizations about personal liberty, freedom of the press, and so on, will not be convincing in most parts of the world. In many areas they will not even be comprehensible. (*Sadly, as true today as when this was written.*)

(b) Since the effect of his own acts is limited, the saboteur may become discouraged unless he feels that he is a member of a large, though unseen, group of saboteurs operating against the enemy or the government of his own country and elsewhere. This can be conveyed indirectly: suggestions which he reads and hears can include observations that a particular technique has been successful in this or that district. Even if the technique is not applicable to his surroundings, another's success will encourage him to attempt similar acts. It can also be conveyed directly: statements praising the effectiveness of simple sabotage can be contrived which will be published by white radio (*Allied propaganda radio broadcasts*), freedom stations (*broadcasts from resistance fighters inside occupied territory*), and the subversive press. Estimates of the proportion of the population engaged in sabotage can be disseminated. Instances of successful sabotage already are being broadcast by white radio and freedom stations, and this should be continued and expanded where compatible with security.

(c) More important than (a) or (b) would be to create a situation in which the citizen-saboteur acquires a sense of responsibility and begins to educate others in simple sabotage.

(2) *Encouraging Destructiveness*

It should be pointed out to the saboteur where the circumstances are suitable, that he is acting in self-defense against the enemy, or retaliating against the enemy for other acts of destruction. A reasonable amount of humor in the presentation of suggestions for simple sabotage will relax tensions of fear.

(a) The saboteur may have to reverse his thinking, and he should be told this in so many words. Where he formerly thought of keeping his tools sharp, he should now let them grow dull; surfaces that formerly were lubricated now should be sanded; normally diligent, he should now be lazy and careless; and so on. Once he is encouraged to think backwards about himself and the objects of his everyday life, the saboteur will see many opportunities in his immediate environment which cannot possibly be seen from a distance. A state of mind should be encouraged that anything can be sabotaged. (*You're thinking about your boss's sandwich in the fridge, aren't you?*)

(b) Among the potential citizen-saboteurs who are to engage in physical destruction, two extreme types may be distinguished. On the one hand, there is the man who is not technically trained and employed (*i.e. the person outside the bureaucracy*). This man needs specific suggestions as to what he can and should destroy as well as details regarding the tools by means of which destruction is accomplished.

(c) At the other extreme is the man who is a technician, such as a lathe operator or an automobile mechanic (*or the career employee trained in the ways of the system who knows the devastating power of a single 'accidentally' forwarded email*). Presumably this man would be able to devise methods of simple sabotage which would be appropriate to his own facilities. However, this man needs to be stimulated to reorient his thinking in the direction of destruction. Specific examples, which need not be from his own field, should accomplish this.

(d) Various media may be used to disseminate suggestions and information regarding simple sabotage. Among the media which may be used, as the immediate situation dictates, are: freedom stations or radio, false or official leaflets. (*Or that social media post with your boss's latest scathing email? Just be wary of attribution. Big Brother knows, if they can be bothered to check who posted what.*) Broadcasts or leaflets may be directed toward specific geographic or occupational areas or they may be general in scope. Finally, agents may be trained in the art of simple sabotage in anticipation of a time when they may be able to communicate this information directly.

(3) *Safety Measures*

(a) The amount of activity carried on by the saboteur will be governed not only by the number of opportunities he sees, but also by the amount of danger he feels. Bad news travels fast (*a universal truth*), and simple sabotage will be discouraged if too many simple saboteurs are arrested.

(b) It should not be difficult to prepare leaflets and other media for the saboteur about the choice of weapons, time, and targets which will insure the saboteur against detection and retaliation. Among such suggestions might be the following:

(*1*) Use materials which appear to be innocent. A knife or a nail file can be carried normally on your person (*Carrying a knife in corporate America is frowned upon these days. Learned that one the hard way.*); either is a multipurpose instrument for creating damage. Matches, pebbles, hair, salt, nails, and dozens of other destructive agents can be carried or kept in your living quarters without exciting any suspicion whatsoever. If you are a worker in a particular trade or industry you can easily carry and keep such things as wrenches, hammers, emery paper, and the like.

(*2*) Try to commit acts for which large numbers of people could be responsible. For instance, if you blow out the wiring in a factory at a central fire box, almost anyone could have done it. On-the-street sabotage after dark, such as you might be able to carry out against a military car or truck, is another example of an act for which it would be impossible to blame you. (*Ghost-pepper hot sauce added to a sandwich is untraceable. Just saying.*)

(*3*) Do not be afraid to commit acts for which you might be blamed directly, so long as you do so rarely, and so long as you have a plausible excuse: you dropped your wrench across an electric circuit because an air raid had kept you up the night before and you were half-dozing at work. Always be profuse in your apologies. Frequently you can "get away" with such acts under the cover of pretending stupidity, ignorance, over-caution, fear of being suspected of sabotage, or weakness and dullness due to undernourishment.

(*4*) After you have committed an act of easy sabotage, resist any temptation to wait around and see what happens. Loiterers arouse suspicion. Of course, there are circumstances when it would be suspicious for you to leave. If you commit sabotage on your job, you should naturally stay at your work.

4. TOOLS, TARGETS, AND TIMING

a. The citizen-saboteur cannot be closely controlled. Nor is it reasonable to expect that simple sabotage can be precisely concentrated on specific types of targets according to the requirements of a concrete military situation. Attempts to control simple sabotage according to developing military factors, moreover, might provide the enemy with intelligence of more or less value in anticipating the date and area of notably intensified or notably slackened military activity.

b. Sabotage suggestions, of course, should be adapted to fit the area where they are to be practiced. Target priorities for general types of situations likewise can be specified, for emphasis at the proper time by the underground press, freedom stations, and cooperating propaganda.

(1) *Under General Conditions*

(a) Simple sabotage is more than malicious mischief, and it should always consist of acts whose results will be detrimental to the materials and manpower of the enemy. (*Bonus points if it's beneficial to the collective office environment. Like that time I discovered that my boss bought two cases of beer with unauthorized government funds 'for entertaining guests' and hid them near my work space. Sure, we could have reported him, but I knew from past experience that such reports went unheeded. Instead, we employees had a delightful Friday night and left the empties for the boss to find.*)

(b) The saboteur should be ingenious in using his everyday equipment. All sorts of weapons will present themselves if he looks at his surroundings in a different light. For example, emery dust—a powerful weapon—may at first seem unobtainable, but if the saboteur were to pulverize an emery knife sharpener or emery wheel with a hammer, he would find himself with a plentiful supply.

(c) The saboteur should never attack targets beyond his capacity or the capacity of his instruments. An inexperienced person should not, for example, attempt to use explosives, but should confine himself to the use of matches and other familiar weapons.

(d) The saboteur should try to damage only objects and materials known to be in use by the enemy or to be destined for early use by the enemy. It will be safe for him to assume that almost any product of heavy industry is destined for enemy use, and that the most efficient fuels and lubricants also are destined for enemy use. Without special knowledge, however, it would be undesirable for him to attempt destruction of food crops or food products. (*This is an important note. In your fight against the system, never do things detrimental to fellow freedom fighters, erm, I mean fellow employees.*)

(e) Although the citizen saboteur may rarely have access to military objects, he should give these preference above all others.

(2) *Prior to a Military Offensive*

During periods which are quiescent in a military sense (*at rest, inactive*), such emphasis as can be given to simple sabotage might well center on industrial production, to lessen the flow of materials and equipment to the enemy. Slashing a rubber tire on an Army truck may be an act of value; spoiling a batch of rubber in the production plant is an act of still more value.

(3) *During a Military Offensive*

(a) Most significant sabotage for an area which is, or is soon destined to be, a theater of combat operations is that whose effects will be direct and immediate. Even if the effects are relatively minor and localized, this type of sabotage is to be preferred to activities whose effects, while widespread, are indirect and delayed.

(*1*) The saboteur should be encouraged to attack transportation facilities of all kinds. Among such facilities are roads, railroads, automobiles, trucks, motorcycles, bicycles, trains, and trams.

(2) Any communications facilities which can be used by the authorities to transmit instructions or morale material should be objects of simple sabotage. These include telephone, telegraph and power systems, radio, newspapers, placards, and public notices.

(3) Critical material, valuable in themselves or necessary to the efficient functioning of transportation and communication, also should become targets for the citizen-saboteur. These may include oil, gasoline, tires, food, and water.

5. SPECIFIC SUGGESTIONS FOR SIMPLE SABOTAGE

a. It will not be possible to evaluate the desirability of simple sabotage in an area without having in mind rather specifically what individual acts and results are embraced by the definition of simple sabotage.

b. A listing of specific acts follows, classified according to types of target. This list is presented as a growing rather than a complete outline of the methods of simple sabotage. As new techniques are developed, or new fields explored, it will be elaborated and expanded.

Author Note: *I decided not to include the next sec-*

tion's highly destructive forms of vandalism which are more appropriate to a full wartime setting (sabotage to destroy roads, commit arson, wreck trains, and so on). While they do make for intriguing reading, they don't fall within my style of satire which explores the human element of surviving within a bureaucracy. If a vandalism guide is what you're looking for, feel free to download your own copy of the Simple Sabotage Field Manual *and join me on the watchlist.*

(1) - (5) *Not included*

(6) *Transportation: Railways*

(a) Passengers

(*1*) Make train travel as inconvenient as possible for enemy personnel. Make mistakes in issuing train tickets, leaving portions of the journey uncovered by the ticket book; issue two tickets for the same seat in the train so that an interesting argument will result; near train time, instead of issuing printed tickets, write them out slowly by hand, prolonging the process until the train is nearly ready to leave or has left the station. On station bulletin boards announcing train arrivals and departures, see that false and misleading information is given about trains bound for enemy destinations.

(2) In trains bound for enemy destinations, attendants should make life as uncomfortable as possible for passengers. See that the food is especially bad, take up tickets after midnight, call all station stops very loudly during the night, handle baggage as noisily as possible during the night, and so on.

(3) See that luggage of enemy personnel is mislaid or unloaded at the wrong stations. Switch address labels on enemy baggage.

(4) Engineers should see that trains run slow or make unscheduled stops for plausible reasons.

(I'm pretty sure that the airline industry has incorporated this entire section of the Simple Sabotage Field Manual *into their standard operating procedures.)*

(b) – (d) *Not included*

(7) *Transportation: Automotive*

(a) Roads. Damage to roads is slow, and therefore impractical as a D-day or near D-day activity.

(1) Change signposts at intersections and forks; the enemy will go the wrong way and it may be miles before he discovers his mistakes. (*Remainder not included.*)

(2) When the enemy asks for directions, give him wrong information. Especially when enemy convoys are in the

neighborhood, truck drivers can spread rumors and give false information about bridges being out, ferries closed, and detours lying ahead.

(3) – *(4) Not included*

(b) Passengers

(1) Bus drivers can go past the stop where the enemy wants to get off. Taxi drivers can waste the enemy's time and make extra money by driving the longest possible route to his destination. (*This happened to me once in London. The cabbie gave a plausible reason for every turn away from our hotel and earned a small fortune for that ride from the airport.*)

(c) – (h) *Not included*

(8) *Not included*

(9) *Communications*

(a) Telephone

(1) At office, hotel, and exchange switchboards delay putting enemy calls through, give them wrong numbers, cut them off "accidentally," or forget to disconnect them so that the line cannot be used again.

(2) Hamper official and especially military business by making at least one telephone call a day to an enemy headquarters; when you get them, tell them you have the wrong

number. Call military or police and make anonymous false reports of fires, air raids, bombs.

(3) – (4) Not included

(b) Telegraph

(1) Delay the transmission and delivery of telegrams to enemy destinations.

(2) Garble telegrams to enemy destinations so that another telegram will have to be sent or a long distance call will have to be made. Sometimes it will be possible to do this by changing a single letter in a word—for example, changing "minimum" to "miximum," so that the person receiving the telegram will not know whether "minimum" or "maximum" is meant.

(c) *Not included*

(d) Mail

(1) Post office employees can see to it that enemy mail is always delayed by one day or more, that it is put in wrong sacks, and so on.

(e) Motion Pictures

(1) Projector operators can ruin newsreels and other enemy propaganda films by bad focusing, speeding up or slowing down the film and by causing frequent breakage in the film.

(*2*) Audiences can ruin enemy propaganda films by applauding to drown the words of the speaker, by coughing loudly, and by talking. (*Anybody who has done Army mandatory training with junior soldiers knows the effectiveness of this technique, especially when the presenter sounds like Paul Harvey reading the back of a cereal box.*)

(*3*) Anyone can break up a showing of an enemy propaganda film by putting two or three dozen moths in a paper bag. Take the bag to the movies with you, put it on the floor in an empty section of the theater as you go in and leave it open. The moths will fly out and climb into the projector beam so that the film will be obscured by fluttering shadows.

(f) Radio

(*1*) Station engineers will find it quite easy to overmodulate transmissions of talks by persons giving enemy propaganda or instructions so that they will sound as if they were talking through a heavy cotton blanket with a mouth full of marbles. (*The modern equivalent of this might be achieved via remixing of social media videos.*)

(*2*) – (*3*) *Not included*

(10) *Not included*

Author Note: *I found the following section the most*

intriguing part of the entire Simple Sabotage Field Manual, *a checklist for how to destroy an organization through ineffective leadership, increased bureaucracy, and strict adherence to The Rules. It ... echoed disturbingly, reflecting the design and administration of the bureaucracies that now run much of our lives. It's almost as though bureaucratic leadership worldwide has long had this chapter as required reading under the heading of 'How to make your employees miserable and laugh while you do it.'*

In Death and the Dragon, *Book 2 of the Grimsworld series, I mentioned a manual in Hell called* The Unhelpful Helpdesk: Hell's Guide to Service With a Smile. *It was a tongue-in-cheek jab at the helpdesk industry, a way to laugh at the insanities we all deal with when trying to get technical support, warranty service, or (heaven forbid) a refund. After reading the* Simple Sabotage Field Manual, *I am now convinced that its closing pages are straight excerpts from another manual written by Hell's Office of Micromanagement:*

Bureaucracy 101: How to Destroy the Human Spirit.

I have experienced every single thing listed below.

Read with care.

(11) General interference with Organizations and Production

(a) Organizations and Conferences

(1) Insist on doing everything through "channels." Never permit shortcuts to be taken in order to expedite decisions.

(2) Make "speeches." Talk as frequently as possible and at great length. Illustrate your "points" by long anecdotes and accounts of personal experiences. Never hesitate to make a few appropriate "patriotic" comments.

(3) When possible, refer all matters to committees for "further study and consideration." Attempt to make the committees as large as possible—never less than five.

(4) Bring up irrelevant issues as frequently as possible.

(5) Haggle over precise wordings of communications, minutes, and resolutions.

(6) Refer back to matters decided upon at the last meeting and attempt to reopen the question of the advisability of that decision.

(7) Advocate "caution." Be "reasonable" and urge your fellow-conferees to be "reasonable" and avoid haste which might result in embarrassments or difficulties later on.

(8) Be worried about the propriety of any decision—raise the question of whether such action as is contemplated lies within the jurisdiction of the group or whether it might conflict with the policy of some higher echelon.

(b) Managers and Supervisors
(*Heavens above, I had flashbacks to some of my worst bosses while transcribing this section.*)

(1) Demand written orders.

(2) "Misunderstand" orders. Ask endless questions or engage in long correspondence about such orders. Quibble over them when you can.

(3) Do everything possible to delay the delivery of orders. Even though parts of an order may be ready beforehand, don't deliver it until it is completely ready.

(4) Don't order new working materials until your current stocks have been virtually exhausted, so that the slightest delay in filling your order will mean a shutdown.

(5) Order high-quality materials which are hard to get. If you don't get them, argue about it. Warn that inferior materials will mean inferior work.

(6) In making work assignments, always sign out the unimportant jobs first. See that the important jobs are

assigned to inefficient workers of poor machines.

(7) Insist on perfect work in relatively unimportant products; send back for refinishing those which have the least flaw. Approve other defective parts whose flaws are not visible to the naked eye.

(8) Make mistakes in routing so that parts and materials will be sent to the wrong place in the plant.

(9) When training new workers, give incomplete or misleading instructions.

(10) To lower morale and with it production, be pleasant to inefficient workers; give them undeserved promotions. Discriminate against efficient workers; complain unjustly about their work.

(11) Hold conferences when there is more critical work to be done.

(12) Multiply paperwork in plausible ways. Start duplicate files.

(13) Multiply the procedures and clearances involved in issuing instructions, paychecks, and so on. See that three people have to approve everything where one would do.

(14) Apply all regulations to the last letter.

(c) Office Workers

(1) Make mistakes in quantities of material when you

are copying orders. Confuse similar names. Use wrong addresses.

(*2*) Prolong correspondence with government bureaus.

(*3*) Misfile essential documents.

(*4*) In making carbon copies, make one too few so that an extra copying job will have to be done.

(*5*) Tell important callers that the boss is busy or talking on another telephone.

(*6*) Hold up mail until the next collection.

(*7*) Spread disturbing rumors that sound like inside dope. (*Okay, I laughed out loud here. Yes, they actually used the phrase 'inside dope' in a top-secret regulation.*)

(d) Employees

(*1*) Work slowly. Think out ways to increase the number of movements necessary on your job; use a light hammer instead of a heavy one, try to make a small wrench do when a big one is necessary, use little force where considerable force is needed, and so on.

(*2*) Contrive as many interruptions to your work as you can (*like that employee who insists on hanging over your cubicle wall and talking about their lunch/vacation/sports team/political party*); when changing the material on which you are working, as you would on a lathe or punch, take needless time to do it. If you are cutting, shaping, or doing other measured work, measure dimensions twice as often as you need to. When you go to the lavatory, spend a longer time there than is necessary. Forget tools so that you will have to go back after them.

(3) Even if you understand the language, pretend not to understand instructions in a foreign tongue. (*I've had coworkers for whom English was a second language who excelled at this task, especially when faced with an idiot boss giving idiot instructions.*)

(4) Pretend that instructions are hard to understand, and ask to have them repeated more than once. Or pretend that you are particularly anxious to do your work, and pester the foreman with unnecessary questions.

(5) Do your work poorly and blame it on bad tools, machinery, or equipment. Complain that these things are preventing you from doing your job right.

(6) Never pass on your skill and experience to a new or less skillful worker.

(7) Snarl up administration in every possible way. Fill out forms illegibly so that they will have to be done over; make mistakes or omit requested information in forms.

(8) If possible, join or help organize a group for present-

ing employee problems to the management. See that the procedures adopted are as inconvenient as possible for the management, involving the presence of a large number of employees at each presentation, entailing more than one meeting for each grievance, bringing up problems which are largely imaginary, and so on.

(*9*) Misroute materials.

(*10*) Mix good parts with unusable scrap and rejected parts.

(12) *General Devices for Lowering Morale and Creating Confusion*

(a) Give lengthy and incomprehensible explanations when questioned.

(b) Report imaginary spies or danger to the Gestapo or police.

(c) Act stupid.

(d) Be as irritable and quarrelsome as possible without getting yourself into trouble.

(e) Misunderstand all sorts of regulations concerning such matters as rationing, transportation, and traffic regulations.

(f) Complain against ersatz (*substitute*) materials.

(g) In public, treat Axis nationals or quislings (*sympa-*

thizers) coldly.

(h) Stop all conversation when Axis nationals or quislings enter a cafe.

(i) Cry and sob hysterically at every occasion, especially when confronted by government clerks.

(j) Boycott all movies, entertainments, concerts, and newspapers which are in any way connected with the quisling authorities.

(k) Do not cooperate in salvage schemes.

—This concludes the excerpts from the Simple Sabotage Field Manual.

Closing thoughts: As mentioned in the introduction, there are no simple solutions to surviving in a bureaucracy. But there are ways to make life there better for yourself and those around you. Regardless of your place in the bureaucratic food chain, consider the methods for destroying an organization outlined in the *Simple Sabotage Field Manual*—then do the opposite. Support your employees and coworkers, train and mentor those who struggle, and reduce bureaucratic burdens whose sole purpose is to feed the machine.

Be approachable and kind.

If you're in leadership, remember above all else that your employees are people. The atrocities of WWII were born from a generation of leaders who lacked empathy, who saw people as only fleshy automatons to be used and discarded. Don't make the same mistake.

If you're a grunt at the bottom of the food chain, suffering under the tyranny of a soulless bureaucracy, remember that you can't fight the system head on. But you can do more than just survive. You can thrive.

Fight the red tape to your dying breath. Just remember to do it snark and style.

Sam and Alvin Bureaucracy join the Grim Reaper himself

in Book 1 of Grimsworld:

Death and the Taxman

https://books2read.com/deathandthetaxman

Thank you for reading *Simple Sabotage: Surviving Bureaucracy with Snark and Style.*

Did you know that book reviews make authors go all soft and gooey inside?

It's true. We love hearing back from readers! Long or short doesn't matter, just share your thoughts.

If you would kindly leave a review on Amazon, Goodreads, or wherever you shop for books, you will have my eternal thanks.

Join the Lost Bard's Letter at https://davidhankins.com for more (free) lighthearted stories.

Acknowledgements

This guide came as a surprise to pretty much everyone, myself included. But even with something that went from inspiration to publication in about six weeks, there were plenty of folks instrumental in getting it done.

Michelle, thank you for adding so much snark, sarcasm, and joy to my life—and for bleeding all over the first draft of this. Your red pen is cherished beyond words.

Beatrix, thank you for being the inspiration behind "Hell's Bureaucracy." On its fourth reprinting now, that's one of my favorite stories.

Wulf Moon and Robert F. Lowell, thanks for the advice over pizza that shaped this guide into what it is.

I have so many soldiers, NCOs, and officers to thank, those who molded my views on leadership, bureaucracy, and the value of perfectly placed sarcasm. To name a few, thank you to: Melissa Parrish, Kristin Burt, Trish Giera,

Ken Tinknell, Jeff James, Cherish Snopko, Don Antonia, Joe Collins, Ashley Millett, and Steven Clark. Never stop being awesome, no matter what life throws at you.

It may seem odd to thank the bosses I didn't like working for, but a commander once told me that everyone has something to teach, even it's an example of what *not* to do. So, thank you to those who gave me the negative examples, even if they weren't the ones you thought you were giving.

Thank you to Sarah Morrison, my illustrator for the Grimsworld series, for helping me give this mad idea a fun cover.

Finally, thank you to all the men and women of the Office of Strategic Service who helped put the original *Simple Sabotage Field Manual* to practical use, helping regular people stand up to tyranny in little but powerful ways. We may never know your specific deeds, but their results have reverberated for generations.

Until next time,

David

About the Author

Award-winning author David Hankins writes from the thriving cornfields of Iowa where he lives with his wife, daughter, and two dragons disguised as cats. His writing began in the oral tradition of convincing his daughter to Go To Sleep with inventive stories. That usually backfired. After years of Just One More Story, David began transcribing his midnight ramblings in an attempt to keep his storylines straight. Children are ruthless about mistakes in their fairy tales. David writes lighthearted stories because that's what he loves to read and—this is the important bit—there's not nearly enough humor in the world. He aims to change that, one story at a time. You can find him at https://davidhankins.com

www.ingramcontent.com/pod-product-compliance
Lightning Source LLC
Chambersburg PA
CBHW071429300726
48976CB00004B/1282